# THE ROT

**The Rot**
**First Edition January 2023**
**Edited By: Christine Morgan**
**Cover Illustration By: Christy Aldridge**
**(Grim Poppy Designs)**

# THE ROT

### STEPHEN COOPER

Splatploitation Press

# Linda Riley

Linda Riley had always been considered a sweet, kind person. One of those people who brought an element of sunshine to any given room. Lightened it up. She was a loving daughter, a warm-hearted wife, and had recently become a caring mum. Little baby Jessica hadn't been planned, but was seen as a gift when Linda and Stewart discovered the pregnancy. They were both in their mid-twenties with decent jobs and a nice small home, so were somewhat set up for the commitment, but even if they weren't, they both knew this was meant to be. Planned or not, the new addition would complete their young, wholesome family.

When baby Jessica's due date was nearing, Linda took time off from her nursing job. She'd stayed on until walking the long halls of the hospital had become too much, and being around the array of sicknesses the hospital had to offer was considered too risky. She'd miss the work, and her colleagues, but she needed to do right by the baby and herself, so took the allotted time off. Jessica arrived nearly two weeks early due to a complication, but both mother and daughter were fine, and after a brief stay at the hospital to make sure they stayed that way, they were allowed to come home.

Jessica was such a beautiful little girl. She had her mum's radiant eyes already. Stewart took a few weeks off from his managerial job to look after them both, and everything felt right. A family unit. A little earlier than they'd dreamt, but that didn't matter. As high school sweethearts, they knew this time would eventually arrive, and it was everything they ever wanted. The future was set, and it was going to be heavenly.

After Stewart headed back to work, Linda began to struggle, something she wasn't used too. Sure, she had her good days and bad days like anyone else, but she'd never felt down for too long. This was different though. She felt sad for reasons she couldn't explain and lacked the energy to do much with her days outside of feeding Jessica. She felt anxious for the first time in her life and even her broken sleep began to feel more ... broken. After confessing her feelings to Stewart, they visited the doctor and Linda was diagnosed with postnatal depression.

The kind doctor reassured her it was nothing to be ashamed of, that it happened to a lot of women and was no reflection of her character. Linda knew this all already of course, but still, she didn't want any negative feelings towards her baby. Jessica was pure and innocent and would be a source of great joy in their lives. She needed this to pass because it was a fucking horrible feeling and unbecoming of who she was.

A couple of weeks after the diagnosis, when Stewart had to return to work again after taking extra weeks off to help around the house, Linda began to feel herself getting better. She had more energy and colour in her cheeks. Some of her radiance had returned. The sadness in the pit of her stomach drifted, a weight lifted. She wasn't completely better; that would take time. But she felt on the mend, and that was the important thing. She felt like her old self again...

...until she didn't.

The sensation was unlike anything Linda had ever experienced, or even seen on the wards at the hospital. Her face felt grimy, filthy. Rotting away! Out of nowhere, like someone had doused her in acid that ate her skin, only with no pain, and no-one to throw the would-be acid. She tried touching her cheeks where the feeling originated, but an altogether different feeling shot to her brain as her fingers ran over the offending spot. The rot felt wet, like soaked plasterboard crumbling beneath her fingers, only no such substance was there when she examined her hands.

Linda rushed to the bathroom mirror and screamed as she saw the effects of her self-diagnosed rot. Her cheeks were flaky, the skin peeled away and hanging. Specks of exfoliated skin dotted across her face like the deterioration was spreading. As if her face was in full blown decay. Impossible! She touched it again. It should have hurt, stung, bled. Anything? But, nothing. It was like prodding a water-soaked surface that was dry. *That made no fucking sense.* Was she having a break down? *God please no*; she thought she was getting better.

It had to be some kind of skin infection? Some fungal shit? But how? When? She watched as the rot spread from her cheeks to cover her nose like a ripple across her face. When it reached her eyes, she thought she'd lose the ability to see as her pupils rolled back in her head, but her vision was fine. Better than fine in fact. Twenty-twenty, which is wasn't beforehand. *Huh.* The rot stopped spreading at her hairline and ears. The texture smoothed out to the point where it melded directly into her skin, leaving no edges or rim to pull it away. *Should she try to pull it off?* Or would her whole face tear away like some old disgusting horror movie? It didn't matter, as she couldn't get a grip anyway.

Linda's screams into the bathroom mirror intensified. She looked like one of the burn victims she'd treated! How was any of this possible? And why was there no pain? Had her nerves been frazzled? Was this real? Surely the answer had to be that she'd fallen asleep and this was some fucked up crazy shit nightmare brought on by the postnatal drugs she'd been taking. But it didn't feel like a dream. It couldn't be real, but it didn't feel like a dream. Then the screams stopped despite her mouth still trying to expel them. Like someone, or something, had hit the mute button. Her hearing briefly felt dulled too, but quickly returned. Whatever was going on there had already passed through.

She felt her face again. This was real all right, or at least real in the not dreaming sense. It still didn't hurt, so some part of her mind reassured her it was just an illusion, some kind of trickery. But why? She wanted to smear cream all over her face, but none of the beauty products she had were built for this. What she needed was skin grafts and facial reconstruction, not fucking face cream. How could she live like this? Her own daughter would be scared of her. Jessica! Linda rushed to the living room as baby Jessica began to stir from her mid-day nap on the living room floor.

*"You want her dead."*

What the fuck was that? Linda started hyperventilating at the cruel words. Her eyes - if they could still be considered hers, as they felt different and were still rolled back - darted round the modest living room. *Who the hell said that? Was someone in her house?* She couldn't see a stranger but it suddenly dawned on her that maybe an intruder had caused this. A ludicrous thought, *how would that even work?* But was it any stranger than it just appearing? Than her face being fucking wet and soggy while being rotten and dry? Fucking nuts.

"Who's there?" she screamed, with the words this time escaping. The bizarre gag order had been reprieved. She twisted and turned, desperate for a better look at whoever had broken into her home. She couldn't spot anyone behind the sofa, and the TV stood within a thin cabinet that was easy to see around. The only other possible hiding place was behind the curtains, but they were wide open. No one here. Linda moved towards Jessica with no other thought except protecting her from a possible intruder when she heard the voice again.

*"You can't deny it."*

Linda didn't recognise the voice as she stopped dead in her tracks, but she did recognise the direction it came from. It came from within. Within her consciousness? Was that right? No. Further. Deeper. It came from her soul. *That couldn't be,* but she knew it was undeniably true. The wretched voice had come from deep within her own fucking soul. That was the truth of it no matter how you sliced it. The voice was evil. That was the only way to describe it without getting poetic about hell. It didn't sound masculine or feminine, just a grumbling evil that was as far from her own voice as possible, yet came from within her. It was an unsettling voice, but one that commanded great power, and contained pure undiluted fucking darkness.

*"She's ruined your life,"* the voice informed Linda with such authority and certainty that it almost felt like fact. But fuck that, it was wrong. Linda shook her head as she looked at Jessica through her tainted eyes. Sweet innocent baby Jessica. The new light of her life. She hadn't ruined anything. She'd brought fresh joy to their already beautiful lives together, the missing piece that they didn't even know was absent. Linda didn't want her dead. She didn't hate or resent her daughter. She loved the baby with all her heart. With all her soul. With every single fibre of her being.

*"You can't lie to me."*

Linda broke down in tears at the statement; it wasn't true. It wasn't. The voice, or whatever the fuck it was talking to her, was full of shit. Total fucking bullshit. She wasn't lying, she loved Jessica. She did.

*"You don't."*

"Shut the fuck up!" Linda screamed, fully waking poor baby Jessica from her in-between state and making the little bundle of joy burst into startled tears. Linda instinctively reached for her, but pulled away. She didn't want whatever was wrong with her face getting anywhere near her baby. If this was some kind of infection, or tactile madness, she didn't want to pass it on to Jessica. Linda closed her eyes, desperate to talk herself out of this horrible nightmare. She needed to wake the fuck up and get a grip. She needed to dunk her fucking head in the sink and baptise herself of whatever delusional evil this was. Linda could feel the darkness stirring inside her, had seen it imprinted on her once flawless pretty face.

*"It would be so easy to break her little scrawny fucking neck,"* the voice told her with an even more vicious tone. The darkness had extra gravel to its voice. The words it spat out came from some kind of hell or demonic land; they weren't words meant to be uttered on this mortal coil. No one wants to break a baby's neck.

*"But you don't want to do that, do you?"*

Finally, something that made sense. Linda shook her head. No she fucking didn't want to do that. The last thing she ever wanted to do was harm her beautiful baby girl.

*"You want something much much worse,"* the voice taunted, making Linda scream again. But this time no noise escaped from her; the mute button had returned. Or was she so terrified the sound got stuck in her throat and couldn't escape?

Linda dropped to her knees as Jessica emitted the scream she so badly wanted to herself. She wanted nothing more than to scoop the little princess up and hold her close to her face, feel that warmth newborns give off. Smell that new baby smell they release. She wanted to kiss Jessica and tell her how beautiful she was, how happy she had made mummy and daddy and how she was the love of her life. But she daren't go near her. She couldn't raise the innocent child to the rot. She left her on the floor crying instead and felt the guilt of her non-action surge through her body. But what was she to do?

*"You want her back inside you."*

The words haunted Linda because there was some truth to them. She missed the feeling of being pregnant. Her body had gotten used to the shared responsibility of looking after two lives. It had almost craved it, and her mood had drastically dropped since the separation. The voice was right, but it was also very very wrong. Jessica was born now. There was no going back. *Was there?*

"*There is,*" it answered, breaking through Linda's resistance. Suddenly she didn't want to scream anymore. She wanted to hear the powerful dark voice out. See what it had to say.

"*She can be inside you again,*" it informed her as fact. A dark evil hellish stone-cold mother-fucking fact.

"How?" Linda whispered, hating herself for even entertaining the notion.

Her decaying face directed her gaze automatically towards the kitchen. More specifically, the oven. Whatever fight Linda had been able to initially put up against this malignant force was waning; she could feel herself slipping away. Worse still, she could feel her will allowing it. *That couldn't be right?* She had to fight it, but she was intrigued by the darkness that had taken hold of her and the suggestion it made. Almost on autopilot she walked to the kitchen, turned the oven on, and cranked the dial to the max while grabbing a baking tray from the cupboard. It all felt natural, like it was the right thing to do. No different from the Sunday roasts she occasionally prepared.

After setting the tray on the kitchen side, she headed back towards Jessica, who was still screaming on the floor. The little rugrat had wet itself only adding to her unhappy noises.

"*She wants to be back inside you, too,*" the voice informed her. "*She's upset at being in this cold dark world.*" The evil had gone from its tone; now it sounded understanding, oddly therapeutic. It felt to Linda like it was giving her helpful advice. Advice she needed to hear and take stock of in order for everything to be better, like it was before Jessica was born. Advice that would make the lingering sadness she'd felt these last few weeks go away. Linda nodded along to the encouraging poisoned words as she scooped Jessica from the floor and settled her on the baking tray in the kitchen.

"Do you want to go back inside mummy?" Linda asked Jessica in that babyish tone new parents used, although she couldn't tell whether she asked it, or the voice buried deep inside her did. *Was there a difference now?* This was what *she* wanted, right? And just as importantly, this was what Jessica wanted. Linda knew that, she could feel it, even if the feeling felt corrupt and wrong. No, they both wanted this. Needed this. It was only natural that mother and daughter were together.

*"This is what you both want,"* the voice reinforced as the rot contained to circle her face.

Linda opened the oven door, instantly feeling the blast of warmth released from it as Jessica continued to cry on the hard baking tray with her little mind not having a fucking clue why she wasn't being picked up and loved.

Then Linda did pick her up, but it wasn't for the love and attention the baby craved, it was to stick her in the fucking pre-heated oven. The hot oven that would feel like a temporary womb again, until Jessica was back inside her.

*"An hour and a half should do it,"* the voice stated, like it was continuing to be super helpful. Linda nodded in agreement as she slid Jessica onto the bottom shelf and closed the door, making sure to set the timer. She'd never been able to work the fucking timer before, but this time she set it with no problems. *A gift from the voice?* Jessica's screams briefly intensified in the oven but didn't last too long, and the oven door muffled a fair bit of the cries anyway. *Quiet at last.*

\*

Ninety minutes later, roasted Jessica was on the table and

Linda was tucking in. *Fuck, the kid tasted good, that was a bonus,* she thought as she split the baby's leg in two and took a big bite from her thigh. With every bite, the baby was closer to fully returning to her mother's tummy. Linda took hungry bite after hungry bite as the voice inside her made yummy sounds. Then, as Linda continued to chew on her precious child, the evil voice faded back to wherever the fuck it came from and the rot around her face melted away to the sound of the front door opening.

"Something smells good," Stewart announced as he hung his coat and kicked off his shoes. "Wasn't expecting dinner on the table," he continued as he entered the kitchen and abruptly stopped. Sitting before him, Linda gnawed on their baby girl, with juices from Jessica's roasted carcass dribbling down her mouth. She looked up at him, readying to welcome him home, when it suddenly hit her what she was doing. She reached for her face but the rot was no longer there. *When did that go? How long had she been eating her baby of her own accord?* Eating her FUCKING BABY!

Linda screamed and cried and hurled on the floor, spluttering pieces of Jessica she was moments ago so desperate to get inside her all over the kitchen tiles. She was finally able to release all the sounds that had built up inside her. She started tearing at her face, trying to find the decay that had made her do this terrible thing, but it wasn't there. *Had it ever been there? Could this have been some kind of mental breakdown?* It had to be. It absolutely fucking had to. She couldn't have done this willingly.

Stewart couldn't scream. He couldn't do anything. What the fuck was he meant to do? He'd got off work a little early, looking forward to some nice family time, and came home to his wife eating their newborn child at the dinner table. He stood stunned while Linda wailed on the floor at a tone he wouldn't have considered possible, although he wasn't hearing it. The world had turned numb. His brain had short circuited. They remained in that state until a neighbour phoned the police after the unbearable noise hadn't relented.

\*

Linda tried to explain to the police about the rot and the evil voice that had somehow taken control of her, but the very notion of it was instantly shot down. At absolute fucking best, she was a crazy cannibalistic schizophrenic; at worst, she wasn't crazy and had done this willingly. She didn't answer any further questions after their disapproving and disbelieving looks. Instead, Linda hanged herself in her cell before she even had the chance to shit the infant out.

No one knew it at the time, but Linda was patient zero. That was where it all began.

# Pearl Irvine

Jerry was snoring again. It had been this way for nearly sixty years and Pearl still couldn't sleep through it when he got too loud. She tried poking him, podding him, nudging him, but all to no avail. She wanted to give him a good old fucking slap, but Jerry was a decent man and didn't deserve that, even if he did snore. When he snored lightly, Pearl could just about sleep through it; maybe not as young lovers, but after growing old together she'd acclimatised. But when it was loud, like shaking the fucking room loud - which most of the time it was - it always woke her and kept her awake. Cherry on top, he had no recollection of it in the morning. *It was a damn good thing she was still madly in love with him after all this time.*

Pearl rolled to her side and checked the glow of the electric clock sitting on her beside table. Her grandkid had asked her what the hell that thing was not too long ago and she was somewhat baffled by the question. Apparently, they barely existed anymore and everyone woke to the sound of their mobiles, at least according to the thirteen-year-old who'd sleep to midday if his mum let him. Fuck that. Pearl was too old for that mobile alarm bullshit. The fact that she'd finally accepted a phone from her daughter was progress enough without it dictating her life. The electric clock had never let her down and the familiar sound of the alarm was part of her morning ritual. She'd woken to that alarm for something like forty years; that wasn't changing.

The clock spelt out an ungodly hour as Jerry's snores somehow got louder. Like he wanted to clue her in on the fact that she wasn't getting back to sleep anytime soon. *No shit Jerry.* Pearl slid her weary bones out of the comfy warm bed and made a beeline for the kitchen, feeling her throat was dry and in the need of a drink. It got that way now that they couldn't leave the

11

window open at night; they both got too cold. So the choice was simple, freeze to death, or wake up with a dry throat. The dry throat option seemed like a better idea, as it meant Jerry could make her a cuppa every morning, as he was always the first out of bed. *No doubt after a good night's unbroken sleep.*

Pearl considered stopping off at the bathroom on her way but thought it made more sense to take a piss after the drink; otherwise, she'd just be getting up again later. She gave Jerry one last nudge after she stood, but he was dead to the world, snoring away at full volume without an ounce of consideration for Pearl's sleeping needs. It couldn't be helped, and he had warned her all those years ago, but still. She wouldn't change a single thing about the honourable man, except the snoring.

Pearl navigated her way round the house without switching the lights on. She didn't need the lights; they'd lived here for most of the sixty years they'd been together, and, barring the odd paint job her son-in-law had given the place, it hadn't changed. She could find her way around blindfolded without holding her arms out if a need to should arise. The kitchen was fucking freezing as-per-usual, which had nothing to do with the windows being opened or not, or even the time of year; it was just a damn cold room. The warmth Pearl had garnered from the bed evaporated quickly.

She opened the fridge door to take the jug of water that had one of those purifiers attached to the top, as the tap water tasted like chalk and needed some kind of treatment. It wasn't that way when they bought the house, but was now. *Progress, my ass.* The alternative was bottled water, but that was too expensive. Not to mention how heavy the bulky bundles it came in were, even if the delivery driver who dropped off their shopping offered to bring it inside the house. *To much faffing about.* It was easier to put the jug under the chalky tap and let the thingamajig do its thing.

Pearl took a glass from alongside the sink and poured the purified water from the jug, taking a nice big gulp before downing the rest. *Definitely going to need the loo before rolling back into bed,* she thought. Pearl went to pour a second glass to the soundtrack of her husband's snores when she noticed something odd in the reflection of the glass jug. Her face didn't quite look like her face. Instead it appeared ... rotten? Decaying? Maybe mixed with some sort of Bell's palsy? It did run in the family. Her face definitely felt like it was sagging though, and more than what the gravity of old age contributed. She went to remove the sleepy dust stuck to her eyes, thinking it was playing tricks on her, but instead felt her eyes scab over. Her knuckles grazed some weird watery texture before her eyesight returned.

*"You've tolerated his fucking snoring for far too long; something needs to be done,"* a mean-spirited voice that wasn't her own told Pearl. She laughed at the statement. It was both correct and preposterous at the same time. Yes, she'd put up with his snoring for a literal lifetime, but the tone and accusation the voice held was ridiculous. It was annoying that he snored, but everything else about him was about as perfect as Pearl could imagine. Like all long term relationships, they'd had their spats, but if the only thing about Jerry she disliked after sixty years was his snoring, then she counted herself a very lucky woman indeed.

*"You're not lucky, you're weak."*

"What?" she questioned. Although who or what her response was aimed at was a mystery. After all this time, had she miraculously fallen asleep to the sounds of his loud snores? That's some progress if so, and why the hell hadn't it happened early in life? But this didn't feel like she was asleep. She'd had many dreams down the years and none had ever felt this real.

*"You're pathetic. Tiptoeing around his snoring."*

"I am not," Pearl countered, annoyed at the accusation while still not knowing with whom she was speaking. It felt like it was to herself, but how did that work?

She checked the reflection in the water jug again; that creepy crumbling look was still there, but no pain accompanied it. The texture was all wrong too. It didn't feel real, despite looking it. *What the hell?* She made her way to the bathroom and pulled the cord to illuminate the bulb, and took stock in the mirror. The rot still hadn't gone, and looked uglier and meaner than it did reflecting in the jug. She could see her mouth and lips, but the rest of her face looked blistered and raw amongst the wrinkles and lines the years had brought her. *What was happening?* She wanted to freak the fuck out and had every right to, except she didn't believe what she was seeing and was too old for such a reaction.

*"You could stick a pillow over his head,"* the voice suggested, like it was on her side - but suffocating her husband wasn't a side she took. What the fuck was this voice talking about? She didn't want to kill Jerry. He was a decent...

*"Decent man... that's what you keep telling yourself."*

"It's true," she argued with her ugly reflection in the mirror.

*"If he was decent he would have done something about the snoring."*

"He's tried."

*"Has he?"*

"He has," Pearl countered, but then wasn't so sure. She thought he had. Didn't he try losing weight to help with it? Although he was fatter than ever now. But she liked bigger men. He took some pills for it once though, or did he? Is that even a thing? Then there was the hypnotist; it worked for his smoking, but not his snoring.

*"He doesn't give a fuck about your sleep. Just his own."*

Was the voice right? It's not like she wanted to believe the evil voice; for starters, it really did sound fucking demonic and the tone it held within every word was far too aggressive for Pearl's taste, even if she really did enjoy a good swear. She liked playfully using curse words, not spraying them out with venom and malevolent intent. But maybe it did have a point. Nearly sixty years of broken sleep was far more than any person should ever have to tolerate, yet she'd not only put up with it, but almost accommodated it

*"Not almost. You have accommodated it."*

Fuck, that devilish voice was right. She had. Why else wouldn't she have given him a good slap earlier when he once again woke her up at silly o'clock in the morning? Like he did every single fucking morning for sixty fucking long sleepless years. What a cunt! And to think, she thought Jerry was a decent man. Honourable. *There's nothing honourable about not letting your wife get some God damn fucking sleep,* she thought with her mind now matching the venomous tone that she had disapproved off mere moments ago.

She stared at the mirror, tracing her fingers around the rot that had infected her face. She watched as the reflection did the same, *like it should,* but it didn't feel like her on the other side of the glass. When the voice spoke to Pearl, her lips didn't move, yet surely this thing staring back was the source of the evil thoughts. No, not evil thoughts, advice. The kick up the backside she needed in order to do something about Jerry. Something about that asshole who selfishly kept her up most nights of the week. That dick who only ever thought about himself. He did bring her a cup of tea every morning and still doted on her after all this time, and looked after her through thick and thin while giving her the life she wanted... but he also fucking snored like a God damn Rhino.

"I should stab him," Pearl told her evil repugnant doppelgänger in the mirror - if that's what the fuck it was? She got lost in the reflection for the moment. She stared at the scabbing across the bottom of her face and her sunken dull eyes with the pupils rolled back like that wrestler her son used to love, and her granddaughter was scared of. *The tall one with the hat.* Her nose looked bent out of shape, but once again didn't feel like it was. The rest of her face appeared to be peeling off, all the way back to her ears. No pain though, and no loose skin when she tried to reach for it. An itch she wanted to scratch, but also felt she didn't need to. An illusion of sorts, although real. There just wasn't... wait... what the fuck was she thinking about again? Oh yeah, stab Jerry!

Pearl tugged on the light cord - practically ripping it from the ceiling, such was her rage - before blindly marching to the kitchen and pulling out the sharpest knife from the knife block resting on the side. She stomped back to the bedroom with a newfound vigour and determination that she hadn't felt in years. Probably because she hadn't had a fucking decent night's sleep in that long! *Fuck you Jerry, you deserve this,* she thought as she reached the room and climbed onto the bed.

Climbing out of bed had been a pain, both in the literal sense, and metaphorical. Her joints had ached, her hip played up, the arthritis in her wrists tingled. Plus the warmth instantly began to leave her once she shed the duvet that shielded her from the cold. Pearl felt none of that now. She climbed onto the bed with ease, like she had her grandkids' energy. She hadn't felt that comfortable in her body since half a life time ago. It felt good. Fucking great even. The voice inside her took a bow, and she couldn't help but smile; the feeling was intoxicating. Absolutely fucking mind-blowing. She wanted more, but needed to attend to something first.

Pearl stopped short of plunging the knife into Jerry's chest and ending the thunderous snores once and for all when she felt the sudden urge to take a piss. In all the hellfire and brimstone upheaval, she'd forgotten she needed the toilet.

*"Maybe it will wake him?"* the voice suggested with a tone that was the sound equivalent of a smirk.

"Maybe it will," Pearl said aloud, flirting back with the wicked voice. She pulled her nighty up and removed her knickers. She was somewhat surprised she could keep her balance standing one-legged on the bed at her age. *Another benefit the voice has bestowed.*

Then she let rip. The piss from her old cunt sprayed all over her grunting ungrateful husband. She aimed for his mouth and nose as he took his overly dramatic deep breaths and continued his uninterrupted sleep. Jesus fucking Christ. Could nothing wake this man?! *Was he that selfish?* Pearl had images of drowning the bastard where he lay, but the piss let up long before that could happen and dribbled down her leg rather than waterboarding him. *Lucky escape*, but she still had the knife.

Jerry continued to sleep, unperturbed by the piss soaking his face and the accompanying smell as it dripped to his nose. The sheets were saturated, but he didn't care. If anything, the snores had gotten louder, but that may have just been in Pearl's head. *Or the voice telling her so.* It didn't matter; it was time to stop the snores once and for all. Pearl dropped from her standing position and straddled Jerry's chest as he remained asleep. The first knife to the gut also didn't wake him, and nor did the second, but the third certainly did the trick.

Blood shot from the stabs across his stomach as Pearl slammed the weapon into him over and over again. Jerry tried rolling her off in his dazed state but he couldn't move. Somewhen within the repeated blows she must have snagged something important, because his body simply wasn't responding to his need to get the fuck out the way. Pearl gave up on his stomach after something like the twentieth stab and tucked the knife into her nighty as something else caught her eye. The glow from the electric clock she'd stared at so many times in the early hours was calling her. She snatched it from the side. pulling the cable from the wall. The numbers blinked off as she slammed the fucking thing against his skull.

*A mobile phone wouldn't cause this sort of damage*, she cruelly thought as the clock broke against Jerry's head, busting him wide open. Blood leaked from the side of his head and joined the piss and sweat on the pillow. The greater cause of concern for Jerry was the blood mixing with the piss lower down, because there was gallons of it pouring from his mutilated stomach. He was surprised he was even aware of it, and even more surprised that his loving, caring wife was the cause of it. He wondered briefly if she'd gone mad, having seen the shit spread across her face. *What the hell was that? Had her face fallen apart?* But it didn't look like madness in her eyes; it was something else entirely. What, he'd never know…

Pearl retook the knife and callously slashed Jerry's throat without a moment's hesitation. More blood sprayed from her husband of sixty years, drowning her in the stuff as his eyes died, along with the rest of his body.

"To death do us part," she coldly said aloud as she continued to stab at his face and neck, not quite done yet. She hacked both of his ears off and stuffed them down his throat. It seemed symbolic to her. Pearl knew the irony would be lost on Jerry, but fuck it, it made her feel better.

In total she must have stabbed him seventy or eighty times before her hands tired. But she wasn't done. Being perched on top of him for this long reminded her of their younger days together, when they would spend a whole weekend in the bedroom, not having to worry about his snoring as they fucked like bunnies. That had been so long ago, and for the first time in a very very long time, Pearl felt wet. It could have been the copious amount of Jerry's blood underneath her, or her own piss, but to hell with it, either way she needed to get herself some.

Raping his corpse seemed only fair after everything that asshole had put her through. Years of sleep abuse. Decades of broken sleep, or no sleep at all. Yeah, he apologised here and there, but actions spoke louder than words. In the end it had been she that put an end to his snoring, not him. Selfish prick. So, fuck him. The least he could do was give her one last good seeing too before his demise, *even if he was already dead.* One last good fuck so that she could fall asleep satisfied and safe in the knowledge that her beauty sleep wouldn't be interrupted. Jerry owned her that much.

*

After suffering his dead, flaccid penis inside her blood-lubricated pussy, Pearl rode Jerry one last time. A last hoorah, before their corpses were discovered several days later by their daughter. Pearl had died in her sleep that night, as the two of them were never meant to be apart. They'd always promised each other in a morbid but loving way that neither could go on without the other. They'd meant it.

The officers on the scene had no fucking idea what to make of what lay before them. The way the scene looked, and what the evidence pointed towards, couldn't possibly be? Could it? The distraught daughter certainly thought it wasn't possible her mum had committed these unspeakably gruesome crimes. It had to have been staged. They all secretly hoped that was the case. That naivety wouldn't last. It was early days; they'd learn.

# Chad Ploughman

Things had been going great for Chad of late. He'd been anxious at first about starting a channel with his girlfriend where he fucked her and another dude on camera - why wouldn't he be, as someone he knew might see it and shame him? - but all such apprehensions had long since passed. They were fucking killing it. Their audience had grown a lot faster than either ever expected and they'd both been able to give up their shitty jobs at the supermarket in favour of running a few more shows daily. *As much as his dick could handle,* they'd joked. Basically, his life was now fucking his beautiful girlfriend and some muscle-bound stud on camera while making more money than he ever had before. He couldn't complain; life was good.

Any initial shame or guilt instantly evaporated when people started liking their performances. The messages came flooding in about how hot his cock was, and how they wanted it. How they loved watching his girl lick his ass while he pounded beefcakes. Chad especially liked the ones about how handsome and gorgeous he was. They swept in from woman and men alike, giving him a massive ego boost and increasing the size of his already charming smile. The positive messages way outnumbered the stupid replies they blocked, and the crude assholes they booted from the comments.

At his day job, all he'd thought about was fucking. The thrill of banging his girl and sucking cock to a live audience while getting paid for it was unlike any other adrenaline rush he'd had in life. Those thoughts got him through his mundane job, and then the awe-inspiring results got him out of the dull employment. They were living by the skin of their teeth, as rent sucked and food cost more without their supermarket discount ... which their former boss was most definitely not giving them after they both abruptly left without giving notice ...but life was on their terms now.

Chad's girlfriend Lola was positioning the camera while he chatted to Kurt. The performances always featured Chad and Lola, but they tended to mix the guy up in their MMF Bi sexual exploits. They didn't know enough willing guys to have a fresh one every day, but they tended to swap every week or so and brought back favourites when it suited everyone's timetable. Kurt was brand new to 'Chad and Lola,' a last minute replacement after their scheduled third wheel got a new job that definitely meant he couldn't risk being fucked in the ass on camera while Lola licked his balls. They paid the third member well each time, but it wasn't constant work and couldn't compete with an actual decent job. The supermarket, yes, but some well-paid high positioned job, nope. Not in a guest spot.

The plan for the evening's performance was simple. The three of them would start by chatting on the bed to their audience, slowly removing their clothes while they waited for the numbers to build. They'd ask a mix of sexual questions and getting to know you ones, all while building the tension in the room as they stripped. Once they had a few thousand viewers, they'd start taking things to the next level. Their formula was normally having Lola blow Chad and the guest for a bit, then give them some of her infamous hand-jobs, all while Chad and the male guest carried on chatting. That would continue for a while until everyone was ready to burst, and that's when the guys began their own fun. Right when the audience was absolutely demanding it, and no one was going to walk away without seeing it. Lola was fucking hot, and had a great pair of tits and a delicious pussy, but anyone visiting their little corner of the site was here to see Chad fuck the guy guest.

And he would. No private room, no pay-wall, no fucking bait and switch, he'd just straight up fuck the shit out of them, and the donations would flood in. It was ridiculous really; if he'd known it was that easy he'd have done this years ago. Only, it wasn't that easy. It was a demanding. tiring job that had taken over their lives. If they weren't performing, they were talking about it, and working out what else they could do within the show. They were keeping themselves in shape to make sure all eyes went to them. They were finding the male guests and making arrangements. They were promoting themselves on various socials while trying to hide it all from their prudish families and so-called friends who wouldn't approve of their 'lifestyles,' while they then had the audacity to moan about their soul-destroying jobs they fucking hated like that was the better option. *Better than getting paid to fuck my super hot girlfriend,* was what Chad wanted to tell them anytime the conversation occurred.

Plus, plenty of other cam couples got nowhere with a similar setup. They made little to nothing and spent most of the their time bitching about the community. But Chad and Lola had something. Whether it was the fact that Chad was hung like a donkey, with washboard abs to die for, or how shameless Lola could be when the guys were fucking, there was just something about their channel that kept their fans coming back. Not only coming back, but paying for it, despite it being free. Sure, they could charge for a private room, but they'd figure that out later. For the moment their formula was working and everyone was happy. And isn't that what life's all about?

Tonight's audience felt like it was going to be a big one to Chad as the evening went on. No one was clicking off the channel when they saw Chad and Kurt sitting next to each other on the bed. with the words Bi-Fuck imprinted at the top of the screen and the sexy little firecracker Lola tucked between them. Both guys already had their shirts off, showing their impressive muscles. while Lola was down to her slinky underwear, laughing at their conversation and stroking their abs.

She'd get to be fucked by both too, but it was a bigger turn on for her watching Chad with the other guy. If she had to make a choice between him fucking her for the rest of her life, or her getting to watch him fuck a bunch of dudes, she'd go for the latter. It got her insanely wet, as the returning audience for Chad and Lola knew well. They'd seen plenty of close-ups of her dripping cunt and heard the groans spilling from her mouth as she watched her man go to town on the fellow guy. They'd seen her rubbing her clit with such ferocity that it had her in tears before collapsing on the bed in a pile of goo, making the kind of noises that got dicks instantly hard and ready to explode.

The messages were coming thick and fast as Lola rubbed both guys' big cocks through their see-through boxers. Plenty of suggestions, praise, and jealousy. Loads of comments about how they 'can't wait to see Kurt choking on Chad's fat cock.' Tips flying in as they readied to watch 'Chad plough Kurt from behind.' They wanted to see him 'jackhammer the beefcake while Lola sucks his dick and licks his balls.' One of their favourites was when Chad would fuck the dude while Lola gave Chad a rim job; they donated the big bucks for that. The biggest tips came when Lola squirted over the dudes while they fucked, and it felt like that kind of night. Everyone was horny and ready to fuck, both sides of the camera. Whether she would do that tonight remained to be seen as it only happened on special occasions.

Lola was flaunting her body in front of the camera while going down on Kurt when Chad first heard the voice. At first he thought it came through the camera, like one of their fans' microphones had somehow overridden something their side and he could hear it. He wasn't the smartest of guys and had zero ability when it came to tech. They'd managed to set the site and camera up with a little help from a friend and now just left it set up and ready to use in their apartment. They'd adjust the position of the camera every now and then and take it off the tripod when they wanted to do closeups, but that's as far as any tech ability went. But the voice wasn't from the camera, or the computer; it was coming from inside Chad. The evil murmur was telling him lies, and he couldn't understand why. He tried his best to keep a straight face on camera while he watched Lola sucking Kurt's dick and making a whole array of yummy sounds, but he didn't hide his confusion well.

*"She could suck better if you smashed all her teeth down her throat,"* the demonic voice suggested, in a supposed helpful manner. It was anything but.

*"Maybe you should grab her head and make sure she can't come up for air. The bitch deserves that."*

*That one wasn't a bad suggestion,* Chad thought, *within reason of course.* The voice meant it literally, but Chad compromised and pushed Lola's head down further onto Kurt's cock, so she was at the base and not far off stuffing his balls down her throat too. She started to gag a little as he held her in place and the money bell chimed repeatedly. Lost in his own little world for a moment, he held her down too long and Lola really did almost gag.

Lola shot him a 'what the fuck look' when he finally let her up for air, but then she tried to play it off like it was sexy and turned her on even more. Her eyes told a different story for anyone watching them instead of gawking at the dribble sliding from her mouth or her magnificent tits swinging about. Kurt was confused too, but also massively enjoyed it. He'd have no problems watching Lola literally choke on his cock. Rather than show any more of her annoyance on camera, Lola moved Chad's head so it was his turn to go down on Kurt. It wasn't the normal order of things, but fuck it, sometimes you've got to mix things up, and he did just take some liberties himself. Like he'd done to her, Lola held his head down as Chad licked Kurt's dick and

24

took it in his mouth to the sound of more chimes in the background. This blowjob would pay for their food shopping tomorrow.

"*Bite it off,*" the voice told him loud and clear. Chad almost answered, except he had a mouthful of cock so couldn't get the words out.

"*Think of the viewers,*" the voice continued. "*No one else on the site would bite it off. You'd be the star attraction. Unique.*"

*Absurd,* Chad thought, *although not wrong.* Still, even someone as dumb and horny as Chad knew you couldn't just bite someone's cock off and get away with it.

"*You should be the one that literally swallows cock, rather than just saying it,*" the evil gravelly voice pitched like it was enjoying itself.

Whatever its intentions were, it had some interesting ideas. Chad mused as he continued to bob up and down, occasionally breaking free of Lola and Kurt's grasp to grab some much needed air. He'd never been one for breathing out of his nose even when giving a blowjob, or eating Lola's pussy, and luckily Lola didn't have his strength to hold him down, while Kurt was only playing. Chad knew the voice was twisted. He could sense the malicious intent behind it and it wasn't exactly hiding its desire to cause pain and make him do some outrageous shit, but there was a macabre allure to it.

Things had been going extremely well on the channel and they were making good money, but in this game you always needed to keep ahead of the curve. You had to have fresh performances and ideas. You needed to push the limits further and further because there was always another couple out there willing to do more extreme shit than you, and it never took long for something to go stale. Fuck, they themselves had stolen a huge share of the market when Lola started squirting over Chad and Eric (at the time). He knew a large portion of their fans tuned in to see that happen again. The excitement of will she or won't she. They'd held back doing it every night to build that very anticipation, but what was to stop another performer doing it nightly? Or something even wilder?

Chad's eyes flicked to the computer sitting by their side. This was their biggest crowd to date, which made him immensely happy, but he saw something else when he looked into the screen too. Something on his face. The camera couldn't pick it up as he was facing away from it, but his face appeared to be crumbling in the laptop's reflection. Rotting. *That better fucking not be happening.* Chad coasted on his looks and the channel demanded he look handsome and hot. No one wanted to watch some dude with a fucked-up face no matter how big his dick was. They could have rebranded, he guessed, like some -kind of freak show. 'Watch the Elephant man fuck guys with this large trunk,' or some bullshit like that, but Chad wasn't ready to be ugly.

*"You're worried about your face?"* The voice sniggered in its hellish tone while addressing his concern. Chad reached for the rot. It felt horrible, wet but dry at the same time. Not the texture he expected. It wasn't right. Wasn't possible. Lola and Kurt hadn't noticed yet, as they chatted to the fans about how many fingers she could take in the ass while Chad continued to suck Kurt's dick.

*"All the more reason to do something memorable now. Get paid while you can,"* the voice teased, but held a certain truth to it. A master manipulator, and Chad couldn't help but begin to fall under its spell.

Chad glanced towards the camera, almost out of instinct. The first message came almost instantly. 'What's wrong with his face?'

*"So it begins,"* the voice laughed, preying on Chad's vanity, *which was all too easy.*

Lola typed about Chad's face being red from all the dick he was sucking, but others started commenting too. Something about his face looking like it was melting? A face like Freddy? Lola didn't have a fucking clue what that meant, so tried checking for herself. Chad kept his face hidden from her as the voice continued to laugh at his predicament, continued to taunt and mock him. But it also offered a way out.

*"Bite his cock off and have some fun, then I'll return you to normal,"* it whispered. The tone was the most sinister thing Chad had ever heard, drenched in blackness, but it had a hypnotic quality to it too, and seemed to be telling the truth. Pure darkness that could be trusted? How was that a thing? But what choice did Chad have as Lola snatched his hair and tugged his head upwards, getting tired of his squirming? She briefly saw the rot as Chad continue to suck cock with his face now in full crystal clear view of the camera and their curious audience. She opened her mouth to say something, but didn't get the words out in time.

CRUNCH.

Chad bit down hard on Kurt's chunky dick.

He didn't think it possible to take the thing off in one bite, but he had. The dismembered prick hung from his mouth with the back end pissing with blood and Kurt howling in pain. The waterworks matched the blood squirts as the pain reverberated around his naked body. The previous granite hard cock went limp in Chad's mouth as the blood made a fast exit. Lola began screaming at him but he'd already blocked her noise out. The money chimed and pinged like crazy in the background, though; that sound he didn't block. Maybe his audience thought this was the best trick ever, or maybe they were a bunch of sick fucks like him? Either way, Chad turned to the camera and showed them the severed penis before chomping down on it and swallowing the cock, just like so many of the channels promised. *Chad fucking delivers.*

He grabbed Lola by the hair and rammed her pretty face into the headboard. busting her dinky nose to more chimes from the donation bell. Fucking payday, just like the voice promised. The evil, sadistic, masochistic voice egged him on further. It told Chad the more extreme he got, the more dings of the bell he'd hear. Chad fucking lived for that chime of late, so the proposition of more definitely got his attention. Lola lay withering on the bed, possibly concussed as she held her busted nose and faded in and out of consciousness while still trying to comprehend what the hell was happening.

Chad turned his attention back to Kurt. He punched him hard in the face several times until he heard the crack of bone under his knuckles. CRACK BING; the sounds of the punch and payday blended together like a beautiful concoction in Chad's warped ears, and a devilish laugh provided a backing track. It took Chad a little by surprise to find it was him laughing and not the voice, but either way it was a sensational symphony of sound. Chad pushed Kurt down onto the mattress and jammed his rock hard donkey cock deep into his ass without warning. Kurt was already in shock and bleeding incessantly so didn't initially registered the harsh penetration until Chad pushed deeper, getting into his guts. *That got his attention.*

Lola lay below the two, unwittingly getting splashed with the remaining blood pouring from the hole where Kurt's dick used to be while her boyfriend went to town fucking him hard and raw. Chad unrelentingly pounded the hell out of Kurt's ass to the soundtrack of bells going off in the background. 'What the fuck?' messages dominated the comments. 'Is this real?' was a close second, overwhelming the page as Chad continued to punish Kurt with everything he had. *A show for the ages,* he thought in his fucked-up head, as the evil cheerleader inside him demand he go *harder and faster.* Lola struggled for breath beneath them as she tried to pull herself out of the compromising position. Blood starting flowing from Kurt's raw ass, adding to the dick blood. Both dripped on Lola's prone, busted face before she finally managed to roll herself from the bodies above her.

Chad released Kurt who slumped forward on the bed, looking like he'd bled out.

*"Either that or you fucked him to death,"* the voice laughed. Chad couldn't help but smile' that sounded like a hell of an achievement if it was true.

*"She's next,"* instructed the demonic voice. Chad didn't need telling, *she* was definitely fucking next.

More questions arose about the rot spreading across Chad's face on the message board, but he'd long since forgotten about that; he was having too much fun. He punched down on Lola beneath him, breaking a bunch of her teeth, and then slammed his fist down a few more times to dispose of the rest like he was getting rid of the remaining glass from a broken window. His knuckles were shredded, and a few broken jagged teeth still clung to Lola's gums, but Chad didn't care. He stuffed his bloody fat cock deep into her throat, ignoring the pain of his dick getting serrated.

Lola couldn't breathe with her small nose heavily busted, teeth down her windpipe, and a massive cock in her mouth. Chad continued to face-fuck her with a look on his own face she'd never seen before. He'd snapped. She could see the rot clearly now, but could also see in Chad's eyes that this wasn't him anymore. Not her Chad. Whatever the fuck had happened to him would remain a mystery to Lola as she choked on the teeth and cock while struggling to find a breath. She died mid face-fuck. That didn't stop Chad.

Once he finished fucking Lola's dead broken face. he moved onto her pussy and ass, all while the payments in the background skyrocketed… at least in his head. He could have just been hearing the chimes in his mind at this point, but the sound kept him going, phantom or not. By the time he finally came over both Kurt and Lola's corpses, his record audience had doubled. He wiped his gory mangled dick on the camera lens and pushed the tripod to the floor as the signal went dead.

*"Now that's what I call a fucking performance,"* the voice crudely remarked before it faded away.

Chad checked his face in the bathroom mirror and saw the rot had disappeared, along with the voice. He had his good looks back as promised. He washed his fucked-up knuckles under the tap, seeing bone as the blood and Kurt meat cleared, and then tried the same thing with his dick. It was messed up beyond all recognition. Lola's broken teeth had sliced the shaft in half like a fucking hotdog and the tip was a bruised swollen mess with parts inadvertently nibbled off. Whatever money he made today would have to go towards reconstructing his pride and joy, if possible.

He was in the shower before the shock of what he'd done finally kicked in, before the memory of *that* voice started to plague his consciousness. He'd been in some kind of trance since the voice left him, but now his actions felt real. The horror and disgust of what he'd done came to the forefront of his mind. Surely it was just some fucked up nightmare? He couldn't have? Never would have? But the bloody bodies of Kurt and his formerly beautiful girlfriend Lola piled on the bed, covered in his blood and cum, told him he fucking had.

\*

\* \* \*

Chad made a run for it after the double murder but it didn't take long for the police to catch him when he drew money from an ATM and was followed on CCTV. He tried explaining the situation, but didn't get anywhere. As far as the police were concerned, he was just some jealous degenerate who killed his girlfriend over some twisted sex tiff. They had no real interest in non-existence voices and face melting, especially when Chad's face looked as handsome as ever. No one watching the performance came forward. As far as they were concerned, some special effects wizardry had taken place, which was cool and all, but they just wanted to watch people fuck. It didn't matter, as the channel never returned. Was some final show.

# Alfie Austin

*"Fucking Niggers"*

"What?" Alfie said aloud, absolutely stunned and mortified by the words. *Did they just come out of his mouth?* There was no-one else in his third story apartment, but he couldn't have said that. Not the N-word. Never. He didn't have a racist bone in his body. He'd never say anything derogatory towards a person of colour, or anyone else for that matter. *Except maybe a Tory.* He wasn't prejudiced towards anybody. He hated all that shit. Each to their own, and respect one another was his motto. *Again, except for Tories, and people with far too much money.* He'd never utter something so appalling. Not a chance. If he had an issue with a black person, it would be something along the lines of the person being an asshole, not anything to do with the colour of their skin. Absolutely fucking not. No. Never. Nope. But yet, there was no-one else in his apartment, so who the fuck said it?

Alife was watching three black people from his window when he heard the words. Two guys and a girl, all around their mid-to-late twenties, were having a conversation outside the local corner shop. They all had smiles on their faces and seemed to be joking about something they'd heard. The girl was really pretty, and that's why Alfie continued to watch them even if it was a little voyeuristic of him. He didn't mean to stare or intrude; he just liked seeing people happy, and these three were very friendly and comfortable around one another. It was something nice to see in a time when there was so much animosity around. Also, as mentioned, the girl was seriously hot.

She had big brown eyes and slight curls in her hair, looking very fashionable and cool. Alfie could easily imagine her being at one of the many protests he'd attended. She looked like an art student, or possibly a photographer or singer. Or maybe Alfie was just hoping she was, filling in the blanks of a possible dream girl. He smiled at the thought of running into her at some gathering, introducing himself and them getting along like a house on fire. He needed to phrase that better. 'A house on fire' sounded far too aggressive despite its supposed kind meaning. There had to be a better way to describe a good friendship that wasn't the cause of so many countless deaths and ruined lives.

He wondered what her name was. The depths of his brain was trying to attach a name to her like Tamara, but that seemed mildly offensive. She could just as easily been a Kate, but she didn't seem like one. She seemed the type of beautiful artistic soulful girl - *woman*, he corrected himself - who deserved a unique name with a strong meaning behind it. Again, was it a little odd thinking like that? Probably not. It only appeared to be white people that didn't give a shit about the meaning behind their names; every other culture in the world seemed far more interested in selecting a name that meant something rather than just whatever ridiculous celebrity or TV character was popular at the time. He was called Alfie before the hundred of thousand other Alfies came along, but that counted for shit now. His name was about as unique as a bottle of milk.

*"They need to go back where they came from."*

"What? Who?" Alfie's eyes darted around the room as the disgusting words broke his thoughts.

"Who the fuck said that?" he uttered aloud. hoping for an answer. Although, if some fucking foul, aggressive, racist piece of shit had broken into his apartment, he probably didn't need an answer. He'd just need a clear path to his front door, and to be dialling for the police from his mobile on the way out.

An answer came, but it didn't come from an asshole bigoted burglar in his apartment; but instead from somewhere much more worrying to Alfie, inside him.

*"Need fucking lynching,"* the voice uttered with such

disgusting disdain it made Alfie want to puke and faint.

"What... That's... What the fuck?" Never in his life had he heard such utter fucking bullshit. Well, maybe not; his uncle was a racist cunt who used to say appalling shit like that, but he'd stopped talking to that dickhead a long time ago. *Is dickhead still allowed?* He'd have to check that.

*"You know you hate them."*

"I do not. That's absurd!"

*"You tell yourself that."*

Where the fuck did this voice get off? Did it know who it was talking to? Alfie didn't hate anyone, other than Tories and Republicans, and Incels, and Trump supporters, and anyone who was knowingly an 'ist' or 'ism'... and the occasional rich person. But those people deserved hate in his mind for being so, well, hateful. But Alfie wasn't one of those people. He was someone who believed in diversity and respect. In free-speech, not to be confused with hate speech, like so many tried to turn it into. He gave a shit about climate change, gender and race issues, and the world he'd be leaving for his future children. He used the correct pronouns and right phrases and made sure he was a loving, respectful, and thoroughly decent human being.

*"Bullshit. You despise those coons"*

"What. The. Actual. Fuck! Who the hell says something like that anymore?"

That was the moment Alfie noticed something unusual in his reflection in the window while he continued to spy on the gorgeous black woman across the street. His face looked flakey, like his skin was melting. He swore he could see the muscles working his jaw, but not in a wet gooey way; more like it'd been that way a while and dried out. Half his pathetic hipster beard had fallen, revealing more redness and rot around his decaying chin and throat as flakes of skin dripped from his deteriorating face.

His eyes were drooping and his nose sliding off. His hands darted upwards, trying to keep the various pieces from falling right off his face like some fucking cartoon from a bygone era. Everything looked dry, but felt wet. His brain couldn't comprehend the difference in look and feel. Seriously, what the fuck was this? He had no idea how his face got the way it was, but could feel a dark power within the rot. A power that was saying those awful things.

*"It's you thinking those thoughts, not me,"* the voice answered, to a question Alfie hadn't asked.

"But I don't..."

*"You don't have to pretend with me."*

"I'm not..."

*"I know what you really want. You want to kill those two drug dealers and rape that black bitch for being the whore she is."*

"No."

The voice started laughing inside Alfie. It was a horrible maniacal laugh. A laugh that suggested it did know the truth, and that every word it just uttered held value. A laugh that suggested it'd tapped into Alfie's deepest darkest secrets and outed him. But that couldn't be? Could it? Yeah, Alfie would love to get in that girl's pants, but rape?

Absolutely not. He wasn't some scumbag rapist. He respected women. Obviously the girl - the woman - was hot; plenty of them were, but he always tried not to objectify them. He wanted to know this beautiful woman, find out her interests, see what made her tick. Alfie wanted to know what her beliefs and aspirations were. He wanted to get to know her friends, and hoped they'd become his friends too. He definitely wanted to know her name; that was the first thing he needed to know about her. And yes, he wanted to kiss her, touch her, run his hands over her body, and one day in the not too distant future hopefully make love to her. But rape her? No. That was wrong.

Wasn't it?

But then... she was a fucking whore.

Wait. What. Is she? When?

*"She's beneath you,"* the voice whispered, in a tone that sounded like the Devil himself was encouraging Alfie, and the Devil would know a thing or two about who deserved what. The voice had an edge to it. A suggestive twang that cut through the bullshit and let Alfie know he could take her. He could own her. He could make this bitch his.

*"She'd like that,"* the unholy voice agreed.

Agreed? Were they Alfie's thoughts? He thought they belonged to the voice, to the rot in the pit of his stomach and the decay spread across his festering mouldy face. He was so confused.

Alfie couldn't wrap his head around why the voice was so right. It made sense when it spoke. Had he been so wrong all this time? Had he been fighting for the enemy? Were the protesters and do-gooders actually the bad guys? No. Wait? That was wrong. They weren't the enemy, of course not. What the fuck was he thinking? They weren't the enemy at all; he just wasn't the nice guy he was pretending to be. They weren't on the wrong side, he was. He was his uncle's nephew after all. *Is that how the phrase went?* It didn't matter.

The voice was right, he should be able to take what he wanted. After all the good he'd done these last few years, like gluing himself to a fucking tree to stop them gentrifying the local park, or protesting that Black Lives Matter and that Trans people had rights. He done his part; now it was his turn to satisfy whatever needs he had. Fair's fair. And what he needed at the moment was his hard white cock balls deep in that hot black slut's worthless cunt. He hadn't even realised how hard he'd gotten thinking about raping that bitch, another sign the voice must be right. Why else would he be so turned on by the idea?

He'd never considered it before, but it made sense now. The voice had opened his eyes, even though the reflection in the window made them look shut. *How could I see?* Didn't matter. It wasn't his eyes that had needed opening, it was his mind. His fucking do-gooding mind. His stupid fucking brain that thought everyone should be equal and that we should live in harmony. Fuck that. Harmony didn't get him the black pussy he wanted. At least, it couldn't at this exact moment, which is where the beauty of just taking it came into play. But first he needed to get her fucking pimps out the way, because no way was he paying for what should rightfully be his.

Fucking glued himself to a tree, what an idiot. Arrested for a sit down to prevent fracking a few cities over. What the hell. Why? All it achieved was put something on his record after they fucking went ahead with it anyway. All those expensive trips he couldn't afford, to march in London over whatever the issue of the week was. What a fucking moron. He'd literally put himself in debt at times, and in return for all that, the skank across the street wouldn't even give him a second look. Like that slut was one to talk. Just look at the way she dressed, asking for it. That's what his uncle used to say, and he should have listened.

Alfie could hear the thoughts spreading throughout his body, the cruel words carrying extra power with them. He wanted to disagree with the nasty rhetoric, but couldn't help but agree. He wanted to shout and scream at the disgusting voice, but found its twisted reverie compelling. He could feel himself being brainwashed, and gave in to it. But the voice wouldn't allow that excuse. It kept telling Alife over and over again that it had nothing to do with it; these were Alfie's own thoughts. His repressed beliefs. The voice simply opened the door he'd tried to keep closed when the world told him it was wrong to think this way. This was Alfie's true self, and people should always be truthful to who they are. *The dimwitted sucker fell for it.*

Alfie grabbed his protest bag from the cupboard. All the peace, love, and respect patches sewn on the bag no longer meant a God-damn thing to him. The diabolical voice had told him the truth, it had uttered it from his very soul. Fuck them all. *He* was the superior of the species. Alfie rummaged through the cupboard for anything else he could use and found his dad's old toolbox, left from when he first moved in. His dad helped put up a couple of shelves, joking about what a pussy Alfie was for not being able to do it himself.

How useless he was. How *his* generation could use their hands. How *his* dad taught him how to fix things around the house and mend a car. How *he* could saw and solder and do all these other practical things that seemed like witchcraft to the snowflakes of today, who couldn't change a fucking lightbulb without a health and safety officer present. Alife's dad wasn't quite his uncle, but he wasn't likeminded to Alfie either. Or maybe he was? Maybe at the time Alfie's mind was just wrong? But it wasn't anymore. The older generation had tried to teach him, but he hadn't listened. Luckily, a new voice had persuaded him to take control. To be a fucking man.

He pulled a screwdriver and claw hammer from the toolbox and shoved a spare hammer and wrench into his backpack before making his way to the front door and down the stairs. When he opened the door at the bottom he could see the girl and two guys across the road still loitering, no doubt planning how to hold up the Paki shop on the corner. He'd have to take them down quick before they pulled out their pieces, or their homies turned up with fucking Uzi's, or whatever the gangs carried nowadays. The streets were awash with these fucking gangbangers and it was up to ordinary decent folks like himself to clean it up. *And to rape their woman.*

And that's what he intended to do.

Alfie grasped the claw hammer in his right hand and the screwdriver in his left as he strutted towards the three criminals. The rot covering his face grew. The infection spread to his ears. The dry skin crumbled and spilt to the floor like dandruff with every step he took. With a face like this, rape was the only way he'd get a girl now anyway. *And he fucking deserved one. This one.* The decay on his face didn't matter for the moment though; no-one could see it in the darkness of the night, not that anyone was looking at him. They were probably all too busy smoking crack and trying to whore their girl's ass out to whatever degenerate towel-head with a tiny dick flashing his daddy's oil money turned up.

The woman caught sight of Alfie just as he reached the trio. She screamed as she noticed the tools in his hand and the aggressive way in which he held them; his intentions were not fucking subtle. She hadn't even noticed his rotting face. Her friends turned to see what the fuss was about but never had the chance to ask. Alfie drove the screwdriver straight into the taller of the pair's ear with strength he didn't realise he had, as it pierced the guy's eardrum and carried on straight to his brain. His whole body short circuited as his eyes rolled back. He was briefly braindead, before he was dead dead.

Alfie swung the claw hammer down on the second guy's head, cracking his skull like a fucking egg while the screwdriver was still sticking from the first guy's brain. As the second guy fell to the floor convulsing from the damage already done, Alfie flipped him over and spread his jaw across the edge of the pavement. Without a second's hesitation, he curb-stomped the asshole. One less dealer and pimp on the street. The girl darted into the shop a blubbering screaming mess as Alfie turned his wicked attention to her.

With tunnel vision he power-walked into the shop after her, his rock-hard dick aching after the satisfying kills. The voice in his head congratulated him for helping clean the streets and now it was time to claim his prize. Not that some nigger slut who'd sucked more dicks than he'd had hot meals was much of a prize, but Alfie wanted her anyway. She was his. She belonged to him now. What his tunnel vision didn't account for was the shopkeeper pulling a metal baseball bat from under the counter and pressing the silent alarm after witnessing the sick attack outside his shop on the CCTV.

The girl screamed as she ran to the back of the shop with tears flooding her face. Alfie's march towards her was cut short just as she'd cornered herself, when the metal bat connected with the back of his legs, dropping him to his knees. After witnessing the vile unprovoked attack outside, the shopkeeper had zero intentions of giving the punk any warning. He needed to neutralise the fucker as quickly as possible, knowing the police were on their way.

He gestured to the frightened girl to get behind him as Alfie stayed on his knees wondering what the hell just hit him. A second swing connected with his jaw, following through to Alfie's head. It knocked Alfie unconscious as the rot infecting his face melted away. Neither the shopkeeper nor the girl noticed the rot's sudden disappearance, as neither saw it when he attacked the two guys and stomped into the shop in the first place. All they could see now were a few missing teeth and a dislocated jaw, courtesy of the bat. The shopkeeper was relived to see Alfie still breathing, as he didn't want a murder on his conscience, but at the same time, if the fucker died from brain swell courtesy of the bat, then so be it. He'd find a way to live with the guilt after what he witnessed the cunt do to those two nice lads outside.

Sirens blared in the distance as Alfie remained knocked the fuck out on the shop floor. The girl rushed outside to her friends but neither was drawing breath. She collapsed, crying on top of them as the shopkeeper kept a watchful eye on Alife.

\*

The papers reported the disgusting unprovoked attack as a hate crime. It was said that Alfie came from a family of racists and had infiltrated several peaceful demonstration groups with the sole purpose of ruining their names, and destroying them from within. He was put on suicide watch after the attacks while he repeatedly told whoever would listen that an evil hostile force had possessed him.

Naturally, no one took pity on the racist murderer, but soon his story would start to become more believable. Whether he'd live long another to clear his name, however, was an entirely different matter.

# Cathy Hill

A flicker of colour entered Cathy's vision. Just black, but that was a colour she'd never seen before. She'd never previously seen any colour. Now this dark colour had invaded her sight... her sight! What a joke. She had no sight, never had. Cathy had been born blind and lived like that for the past twenty-six years, but now she could see something. Black. Darkness. A darkness caused by a darkness, but she didn't care about that for the moment. The important thing was she could *see* the blackness in front of her, and then it turned to white. Two colours. Two colours she'd never seen before in her entire life. Her whole body was tingling, trembling uncontrollably. The sensation was almost too much to bear, but at the same time she didn't want to lose the moment. She wanted to live in it forever.

The white turned to light, then remarkably to *vision*. She could see in front of her as she walked down the long country road that led to the town centre. She'd walked this road so many times in her life, knew it like the back of her hand, but both were just through touch. Cathy knew the smell of the walk, the potholes in the road and pavement. She knew where the few traffic lights were, could time each part of her journey to them knowing what was coming despite never seeing it. But now, she could see it.

A tree stood before her as clear as day. It was impossible, but the gravelly voice inside her told Cathy it could make it happen. At a price of course, but there was no cost Cathy wasn't willing to pay to see the rest of the trek. To see the path and roadside. To see the trees and bushes. Maybe catch sight of one of those cheeky squirrels that occasionally ran across her feet, although it was the wrong time of year for that. Maybe she could put a face to the voices that talked to her along the route? Admire Mrs Colt's dog rather than just carefully run her hand over his beautiful fur.

Tears trickled down Cathy's face underneath the sunglasses she used to hide her inadequate eyes. This was a miracle she'd given up believing possible a long time ago. She had been told she'd never see, that unfortunately there was no hope, but Cathy had hope. She had hope for the longest time that something would change, but it didn't. Like the doctors told her parents at birth, Cathy would be blind for her entire life. She was the last person to accept it, but as she got older and became aware of the situation, she finally did. She given up hope, until now.

'Can't miss what you've never had,' was a phrase she'd heard all too often in life. It wasn't meant as an insult, or with malice, but fuck everyone who said it. It was easy for them to think that. They'd seen their parents, recognised their brothers, sisters, and friends. They'd watched movies, gone to shows, and glimpsed the faces and smiles of cute guys checking them out. Cathy had been told she was pretty, but how the hell was she meant to know if that was true or not? She didn't even have anything to judge it by. When she questioned this she was told, 'beauty is on the inside.' Everyone apparently had a stupid fucking saying for everything.

A car drove by as Cathy gawked at the stately tree. She could see through the corner of her glasses the driver staring at her cane as he watched her stopped in the middle of the path. She'd touched enough faces to piece together the look, it was one of pity. Another thing she'd had to put up with her entire life. Cathy was independent, she lived by herself and her mum checked in on her every now and then, but she didn't resent the pity the driver showed her. He felt bad for her, and she felt the same. Life was tough even with the power of sight.

Now that she'd seen a couple of the things she'd been missing out on her entire life, it was no wonder people pitied the blind. Sure, she could be angry at them for looking down on her, but whatever way Cathy or others tried to twist it, she was missing out. This single tree brought her more happiness than anything else she'd felt in her life. More happiness than her favourite music, or first kiss. More joy than a deliciously cooked meal, or an evening with friends. The sight of the proud tree represented her wildest dreams come true.

*"Didn't I tell you I could make it happen?"* the corrupt voice told Cathy as she continued to watch in awe at the brown leaves swathing in the wind. They were beautiful. What a sight, for her first. She didn't recognise the colours of brown, orange, and red, but fuck, they melted into each other so majestically. And they were meant to look more beautiful and colourful in spring; *how was that even possible?* The trickle of happy tears continued to flow as her eyes traced the bark of the tree, taking in every single minute detail.

Her eyes briefly left the tree to the stone wall that ran alongside the path. A wall she'd held on to many times; it didn't look like she thought it would. Its texture was rough and looked old. The wall was crumbling, something she'd never thought about, as to her it was sturdy and reliable when called upon in precarious moments. She'd run her hand over the top of the wall her whole life without knowing the battering and struggles it took at the hands of the elements. It was still standing though.

"It's all so beautiful," Cathy ecstatically stated. Her eyes wide, and all consuming. She had to take in every second of this, record every single detail to memory. "Thank you so much," she cried happily to the voice inside her. No one had ever given her a gift like this, how could they? This was impossible. She'd been told over and over to the point of frustration on many people's behalf that she'd never see, yet... here she was looking at a majestic tree. Seeing it with her own two eyes. Admiring its beauty. Staring at the dependable stony wall in front of it and the magnificent sky above. It didn't matter that the day was grey and overcast; she'd never seen that before either. It was all new and picturesque to Cathy. She had been missing out. No matter what people said, or the lies she told herself to keep from depression, she had been missing out. Now that she'd seen through the looking glass, she had to keep it. She couldn't lose the sight that she'd spent a lifetime praying for.

"And all I have to do to keep my sight is kill?" Cathy questioned.

The voice inside Cathy had made the proposal before it restored her sight. It'd been thin on the details, but the promise of sight left a lot of wiggle room. She'd do whatever it wanted, even more so now that she'd caught a glimpse and knew this was just the tip of the iceberg. A tree, a bush, a stone wall, the sky, a car. That was nothing, less than one percent of the things to see. She continued to walk as she listened to the scheming voice buried deep inside her. She used her stick as to not raise any suspicion, like the voice commanded, despite the urge to run around freely and take full advantage of what'd been given. But there was a lot to do, and if Cathy played this right she could get everything she ever wanted, the voice had suggested.

At the corner of the country road, a round mirror sat beside a sign helping drivers navigate a sharp bend on the single lane that lead to the village shops. Cathy looked up at her reflection in the round mirror. It was a little distorted, but that didn't matter as she saw herself for the first time in her life. She traced the rot at the bottom of her face running up to her cheeks. It looked like her face was falling apart, crumbling like the old stone wall. No one had ever mentioned that before. It didn't look particularly beautiful to Cathy in her limited experience, but she guessed it was pretty easy to lie to a blind girl in order to make her feel better.

She left the sunglasses on, not wanting to see the eyes that had forever betrayed her; they could wait. Instead, she checked out the rest of her body through the warped mirror. She had a nice figure, something she'd run her hands over a lot during her adult life, but seeing it was something altogether more. She couldn't help but touch herself as she ran her hands over every part of her body, watching the reflection with pure fascination as she did.

"You ok there, Cathy?" a chirpy voice asked behind her. It belonged to Tom, an old farmer from around the area, who often walked the same route to the village as Cathy and always said hello to her.

"Thought I'd lost my keys," Cathy quickly replied, with the lightning wit she was known for, and thank fuck for it because she knew exactly what it looked like she was doing.

"You need a hand round the corner? Haven't lost your bearings have you?" Tom asked with genuine kindness in his thick country accent. He wasn't treating her like a child, or lesser, just a helping hand if need be. She'd always liked Tom, he had a kind voice. It took everything she had not to give away the fact that she could see him for the first time and noticed that a friendly authentic smile came with the kind voice. She wanted to give him a great big warm hug.

"*Lets start with him,*" the voice demanded, sensing Cathy's affection towards the old man.

There had been hints of its evilness almost immediately but Cathy ignored them. They'd been easy to look past in the excitement of what it was offering. Now the sick, twisted side of the demonic voice was clear as day, its sadistic nature obvious in every syllable passed from its vindictive tone. A voice not to be fucked with, especially when it held all the power.

"*Hit him with the rock when he turns away.*"

Cathy could see the rock the voice meant. It sat proudly on

the stone wall. A marker for the halfway point of her journey. Not officially of course, but for Cathy it was. She paid attention to these sort of details even if no one else did.

"But, I like him," Cathy told the voice, as a matter of fact rather than anything too argumentative.

"What was that love?" Tom asked, not quite catching what she said.

*"We have a deal."*

They did have a deal, and while Tom was a warm-hearted lovely human being, he wasn't sight. He wasn't a miracle. He wasn't a life changing event, although killing him could be. Killing him could potentially restore her sight forever. *An eye for an eye*, Cathy and the voice both thought at the same time. It could have been a sweet moment, if they weren't talking about murder, and one of them wasn't the very essence of unbridled evil.

"I'm ok, Tom," she managed to utter while her trembling lips gave away that she wasn't. Fortunately that was a detail Tom was never going to pick up on. His hearing wasn't what it used to be, and ironically neither was his sight. Age could do that to you, but he wouldn't have to worry about that much longer if the Rot got its way.

He said his goodbyes and told Cathy if he saw her in the village maybe they could grab a slice of cake together from the bakery, his treat. Cathy smiled at the suggestion and then smashed Tom over the head with the rock the moment he turned his back on her. He stumbled forward and fell in immense pain and shock as the large rock smashed against the back of his cranium, splitting the back of his head open. Cathy didn't know she possessed such power, but then anything seemed possible today. She quickly mounted Tom as he lay stunned on the ground, managing to turn over and see it was Cathy who attacked him. Even with her being the only one around and having just been talking to her, he still wouldn't have guessed it. He tried bringing his arms up to protect his head but Cathy brought the rock down again, this time crushing the front of his face as Tom's frail arms did little to deflect the blow than snap themselves.

His nose folded inwards. That nose she'd only seen for the first time moments ago, despite knowing Tom practically her whole life. The next blow closed his right eye. *Now he'd know how she felt,* especially when the edge of the rock bashed into the left one too. The fourth and fifth shots fully broke open his forehead and ended his life. If the rock had taken his sight, he didn't have to live with it for long, unlike Cathy. *Lucky bastard.* She tossed the rock over the wall running along the pathway, and then dumped Tom's body carelessly over it too.

She'd seen a whole new array of colour during the attack as red burst from every part of Tom's broken face. A green and yellow pus had squirted from his eye as it ruptured and leaked. White dribbled from his mouth as he choked on his own blood and his teeth crumbled under the blows. It was like seeing a painting for the first time. So many colours mixing and changing. Was this art? If it was, Cathy had created her first piece.

The voice egged her on the whole time. With each smash of the rock, it shouted for another, but she didn't need telling. If it meant she could see and keep her vision, then Cathy didn't need the encouragement; she'd do whatever necessary. A sad truth that many would feel ashamed to admit, but you only get one chance at life. She'd heard that phrase before as well, and at this precise moment she was taking that one literally and seizing the opportunity. Tom didn't deserve to die, but she didn't deserve to be blind.

Cathy used her feet to brush Tom's blood and skull fragments from the ground beneath her but luckily it wasn't too visible anyway. The fallen leaves from the trees lining the walk already hid half the mess and Cathy pushed more of them over the gruesome murder scene, obscuring most of the evidence. Dollops of mud hid even more as the red blood mixed with the brown dirt coating the pathway. If someone looked hard there was plenty of evidence to point towards something nefarious, but at a glance the ground just looked grubby.

*"You liked that."*

"I like seeing."

*"You can't lie to me."*

"Who are you?"

*"Would you believe, your soul?"*

It was something Cathy could believe. She'd often stated to herself how she'd do anything to be able to see, even just for a day, but she doubted her soul actually had the ability to make that happen. *So what if I did like it?* Cathy didn't need to say it aloud; the voice already knew. Whether it was pent up frustration, rage at the world, or just a deep buried evil inside her, she enjoyed destroying Tom's face, even if he was kind. He'd lived his life, something she hadn't had a chance to do. Yes, she got up each day and did stuff, but she could never live the way she wanted. She bet Tom had never stopped and admired the tree the way she just had. If he had, it would have been a long long time ago. Now, seeing things meant nothing to him. But for Cathy, it was everything. *Something worth killing for.*

Further along the road, Cathy crossed paths with Mrs Colt and her fluffy dog and promptly killed them both. She didn't want to kill the dog, but the voice threatened to take away her sight if she refused. Cathy didn't like being held to ransom, but the annoyance faded when she felt the dog's neck snap under the weight of her cane she'd use to beat it with. The crack sounded good. Unlike Tom, Mrs Colt had noticed the rot on Cathy's face and asked her about it. That's when the voice told her to attack and Cathy wasted no time doing just that. But did it mean the 'rot' wasn't normally there? She didn't know, but no one had ever brought it up before; maybe it was another price paid for the ability to see. Once again, she considered it a fair deal.

The wall had stopped by that point in the journey but there were enough thick bushes along the path to hide the two bodies. She'd absolutely gone to town on Mrs Colt's. She'd whacked the hell out of it with her cane before wrapping her hands around the woman's neck as her dog whimpered and died alongside her after receiving multiple shots with the cane to its cute little noggin itself. She really wished she didn't have to kill the dog, but what was an animal's life compared to her sight? During the brutal assault, Mrs Colt's coat had half come off and her dress had ripped, revealing one of her tits as she struggled to buck Cathy off her. Another new sight for Cathy, and one that reminded her to check her own out. She'd touched them enough, about fucking time she got to see them.

The diabolical voice again congratulated her on the attack. It sounded like it enjoyed it a little too much, but Cathy understood the feeling; she felt it too. Taking someone's life was a powerful, unforgettable act, but seeing herself do it was something all together more intense. Witnessing Mrs Colt's jaw dislodge and knowing she'd caused it sent a rush through Cathy's body. The way her right arm buckled and broke as Cathy leant down on it was a thrill she'd never experienced before. She looked on in awe as blood trickled from the damage caused to Mrs Colt's orbital bones at her hands. She'd seen the different shades of purple and blue darken as she held her hands tightly round her neck and watched each individual breath, waiting to see which one would be the last. Actually watched. Not felt, not imagined, but seen!

Cathy killed her third and fourth victims on the walk when

she destroyed a kid on his way home from the village, and then the postman, who rode his bike in these parts and, like Tom, always stopped to say hello. She'd brained the measly little kid, who had no idea how privileged he was to be able to see from birth, and choked the postman with the wheel of his own bike after taking out the back of his legs with her cane. Not a single one of them had the slightest inkling of what was coming. Duped by their own ignorance of her 'condition.' *Where was their fucking pity now?!*

Even with the decay on her face and blood on her clothes, none of them had a clue. It was so straightforward to lie to each and every one of them. Tell them she'd fallen over. Tripped. Such concern and sympathy flashed across their faces. Not the slightest question of why so much blood? Or, how the fuck did it get in your hair? They just wanted to help. Idiots. So easily tricked... but they weren't the only ones.

As the village came into sight - *and what a fucking sight it was to behold!* - suddenly Cathy's view of it faded. She could longer see the buildings and thatched roofs, the sky above or the nature surrounding. She couldn't see the browns, yellows, oranges and reds of the trees. The white and black that first entered her vision were also gone. All the colours disappeared in the blink of an eye. She asked the voice what the fuck was going on, but it didn't answer. She stood panicked at the lack of sight. Despite it being her norm for so long it suddenly felt alien and scary. *This can't be happening.* She asked over and over, demanded it brought her sight back, but there wasn't the slightest peep from the dark evil voice. She couldn't feel it inside her anymore, and her face had returned to normal.

Knowing she was covered in blood with a trail of hidden bodies she'd killed behind her, Cathy decided to forgo town for the day. Instead, she headed back to her small little home, showered and changed clothes. She got rid of her normal cane and replaced it with a spare. The emotions running through her felt too much to process, but she now knew several things about herself after the miraculous day. Firstly, she was a murderer, and was surprisingly ok with that. She suspected the voice had somehow manipulated her, but she didn't feel like it took over her completely. There had always been a literal darkness in her life, but it spread further than sight. The resentment and rage had taken hold of Cathy and she allowed it. She wanted it.

Secondly, the gift of sight was the single greatest moment of her life. The voice had lied to her, or at least told a half-truth in saying she could have her sight. She guessed it was her who assumed it meant permanently. Cathy was pissed off beyond all belief to lose it, but overwhelmed to have had it in the first place. She wanted it back now that she knew it was possible. Whatever the voice was, and she strongly suspected it was some dark devilish old evil possibly from the very depths of hell, she thanked it for allowing her to see, and wished that one day it would return and restore her sight once more. In return, she'd gladly kill for it.

# Ben Hutton

On almost any given day, school sucked for Ben; it just wasn't his thing. Unfortunately, at thirteen-years-old, he still had a couple of years left of the shit show. He hated almost every lesson, except art, yet art was the subject that got him into the most trouble due to the 'erotic' nature of a lot of his drawings. The kid was obsessed with panties. It wasn't even a sexual thing to begin with; he just liked the different types and colours they came in. But the older he got, the weirder it became for everyone around him. His 'pantsu' drawings had become problematic, rather than just a childish phase.

His parents had been called into the school several times for his 'pornography material' and eventually he had to stop drawing them through fear of suspension, or a fucking beating from his old man. He tried explaining to them it wasn't porn; he barely knew what porn was when they first brought the subject up ... although he was a fucking expert on it now. But his point being, it wasn't porn, it was art, just a fun hobby he enjoyed. That defence didn't stand and he was abruptly told to stop drawing panties immediately and that he was making the female students and teachers uncomfortable.

While that could have mostly been true, Ben believed one of the girls in his English class was 'begging for it,' as his older sister Carly's dickhead boyfriend Brad was fond of saying. Nikki often sat opposite Ben in English and always had her knickers showing as she sat with her legs apart and her short skirt not entirely covering her panties. Ben's best mate Shane also noticed the cute undies on multiple occasions but never drew them like Ben, just admired them from across the classroom. It pained Ben that he couldn't immediately draw them anymore through fear of getting caught and suspended, not to mention the ass-whipping he'd receive from his father.

But he could make a note of the colour and type and secretly draw her in them from memory when he got home ... after he whacked off to the mental image, of course. *So there was that at least.*

The reason school hadn't entirely sucked for Ben today was once again Nikki had sat opposite him and worn a cute pair of pink flowery knickers that she had no problem flashing in his direction. 'She's a sort,' Carly's asswipe boyfriend would say, and Ben wondered if he was right. Especially when Nikki told him at the end of class she expected to see a drawing if he was going to spend all lesson staring between her legs, which is exactly what he'd done. *He thought he'd been subtle about it, but apparently not.* She'd gone even further after that initial remark and caught up with him on the way home from school, and handed him the pair of knickers she was wearing. "So you get it right," she told him without stopping as she ran on ahead after the knicker baton exchange. Yep, most days at school absolutely fucking sucked, but this wasn't one of them. This may have been the best day of school ever, maybe of Ben's entire life.

Ben almost told Shane about Nikki's panties being in his possession but wanted to enjoy them for himself first. *No telling what that degenerate would do to them.* Shane was the kid who'd introduced Ben to porn after the initial accusation, and well, that kid was into some fucked up shit, courtesy of having three older brothers - one of whom had once supposedly fucked Ben's sister. She'd denied it when he questioned her about it, and called him a little fucking pervert for even asking, but Ben suspected it was true. He'd heard Carly and Brad going at it anytime their parents left the house and he'd seen how often Brad snuck through her window and stayed over without their parents knowing. He'd watched them fuck through the keyhole on her bedroom door on more occasions than he could remember, so she 'seemed the type' that would have fucked

Shane's older brother, as that douchebag Brad would say. More so, if the rumour was true, she'd done it while dating that loser, which amused Ben greatly, knowing Brad's fragile posey ego.

Apparently, according to Shane's brother, Ben's sister liked it in the ass, but he'd never seen her and Brad do that. He'd seen plenty of other girls being fucked in the ass on the internet, but none in real life. Shane had told him anal was way better than pussy, but he doubted Shane had ever experienced either. None of the girls in school ever took any interest in him, but according to Shane he was very popular at another nearby school and had fucked half the girls in year nine. Ben pretended to believe him, but knew in all likely-hood Shane was a virgin just like him.

Although, Ben had to consider the fact that maybe he was one step closer to losing that virginity today after Nikki handed over her panties. Sure, they were for drawing, and he knew she loved Anime, so maybe that's why she liked his doodles way more than the other girls in his year, but it might *also* be because she had a thing for him. He certainly hoped she did, as he'd love to fuck her, be it the pussy or ass. Maybe she'd even suck his dick. He'd seen his sister do that to Brad every time they'd fucked so figured it had to be a big part of the whole sex thing, and the girls on his computer enjoyed it.

When Ben got back from school, only Carly was home. His parents were out for the evening and had left pizza money, meaning they'd be gone for most of the night, while that butt-head Brad was working a late shift so wouldn't be around anytime soon. Carly stayed in her room doing whatever girly shit she was up to, so Ben had plenty of privacy to sit on his bed with Nikki's cute pink knickers laid out in front of him and his pencil and paper at the ready. Before he got to work though, *he needed to get to work.*

Ben sniffed the panties when a voice entered his head. The voice sounded like something from one of the horror movies

Shane's oldest brother had shown them. Demonic in nature, but not entirely unfriendly. One of those voices that you shouldn't trust, but so often the dumb kid in the horror flick did.

*"They smell good?"* the voice quizzed.

Ben looked around the room, worried that his dad had come home, or Brad had turned up early, but his door was closed and no-one was around.

*"Go ahead, sniff them again,"* the voice encouraged. So Ben did.

They smelled lovely in Ben's opinion, much better than his sister's. Ben and Shane had regularly smelt her undies after stealing them from the washing basket and replacing them before anyone knew. His sister's panties always had a more sour smell to them. Maybe that was a bit harsh, but he didn't have the vocabulary to accurately describe it, and they did belong to his annoying older sister. Whatever the word, they weren't as sweet smelling as Nikki's. Maybe it had something to do with her being younger? In all the pornos he'd watched, the girls always pretended to be younger than they were, so it was obviously important.

Ben could feel himself getting an erection. It was a relatively new sensation in his life, but he fucking loved it. Some kids his age might have been embarrassed by it, but Ben would have it as his default state if possible. He reached into his boxers and began tugging at his cock.

*"That seems like a waste,"* the sinister voice stated, and Ben couldn't help but agree. It did seem like a waste, but what else could he do? Maybe after he'd drawn the picture he could invite Nikki around if she liked it, and then see what else she liked? But that wasn't an option at the moment.

*"She might not be around, but someone else is."*

"I've wanked over her plenty," Ben truthfully answered. Every time he'd watched his sister suck or fuck Brad, he'd sprinted back to his room and squirted jizz all over his tummy. It didn't matter that it was his sister he'd been watching. Tits were tits, and pussy's pussy, any of Shane's older brothers, or Shane himself, would say. That Neanderthal Brad would cheerfully tell him 'any hole's a goal' with a shit-eating smirk on his face. Ben always thought they all sounded a bit douchey, but that didn't stop him copying them when the situation required it, which was basically any time he was around any of them.

*"Maybe you could do more than just wank over her?"* the voice enquired. Ben was intrigued. What did the creepy sounding voice mean? He'd touched his sister's tits once when she was asleep on the sofa, while playing truth or dare with Shane, but that whole experience had been far too nerve-wracking. He hadn't even got to enjoy feeling her up despite getting away with it and her not waking. It should have been one of the greatest moments in his young life, but honestly, he was more worried that she'd fucking kill him. Again, that didn't stop him later having a wank over the memory, but it wasn't the same as doing it right after. Luckily he got Shane back by making him moon his neighbour's cat, who proceeded to scratch the hell out of his ass. That put an end to truth or dare for a while.

*"You want to fuck her?"* the voice asked as a genuine question. Ben felt a little embarrassed. He didn't understand what the voice was, but it felt like it was coming from inside him, that it would know if he was lying. If he was truly honest with himself, the answer was yes. Carly was seventeen years old and had a great body. Her tits looked as good as any of the girls online and her pussy was always shaven like them too. He wasn't a fan of the smell of it in knicker form, but maybe it smelt different up close, and he had to admit he wouldn't mind finding out. But she'd never go for it. She had that shitface Brad wrapped around her little finger, and his dick was at least four times the size of Ben's, more like the cocks in the videos he watched with Shane.

Ben knew his would get bigger as he got older, but that wasn't going to happen by the end of the night.

"*Size doesn't matter,*" the voice told him. "*It's what you do with it.*"

"You think she'd let me?"

"*Isn't up to her.*"

"Really?"

"*Really,*" the voice replied, with an extra thick layer of malice that chilled Ben to the bone. But he ignored the chill, especially if it meant he could have sex for the first time. With a hot girl too, not some skank that Shane's second oldest brother would fuck. He'd seen the state of the girls he brought home; Shane and him would laugh all night long about them on sleepovers. Although both would have been balls deep in them given the chance.

"*Just with a bag over their head,*" the voice joked, making Ben giggle.

"Exactly," he told the voice, like they were buddies.

"So," Ben anxiously began, "How would I do it?"

"*Smack her over the head and fuck her brains out*"

Ben laughed. The voice suddenly seemed silly, but... "Would that work?"

"*If you hit her hard enough.*"

"I don't want to hurt her," Ben replied.

Carly was fucking infuriating at times, and always gave him shit about his drawings, threatening to murder him if he ever drew her knickers - which he had done at least fifty times without her knowing - but she was still his big sister. She still covered for him if he got into other kinds of trouble, and rented him movies he wasn't old enough to watch. She defended him whenever Dad lost his shit over something he'd done and threatened to put Ben over his knee. She even beat up Dean Knotts after he'd stolen Ben's backpack and pushed him to the floor. She'd done a right number on the biggest bully in Ben's year, another reason to probably not fuck with her, in the literal and figurative sense.

*"She'll forgive you."*

"Really?" Ben didn't seem so sure. Whenever she threatened him it always felt like she meant it. And then there was Dad, he probably wouldn't be too happy about him attacking his sister either. He hated it when they fought, and always told them they should look out for each other. It's why he forgave her every time she came to Ben's rescue whenever he was about to teach the brat some manners.

*"If you hit her hard enough on the head she won't even remember."*

Ben had heard about things like that; it happened in action movies all the time. "Ambrosia," he said aloud. *Close enough,* the voice thought.

*"You won't kill her, just knock her out a little,"* the voice reassured.

Ben could feel his erection swelling like never before. He was actually going to get to fuck someone. Lose his V plates, as the girls in his year would say. *Shane's going to be so jealous.* Ben looked around his bedroom for something he could use to knock Carly out with. She wasn't the biggest girl; by the end of the year he'd probably be taller than her, but she was scrappy. He needed something that wouldn't hurt her too badly either. Nothing permanent. Deep down he loved his sister; he just needed to borrow her for a while. His eyes fell on a cricket bat in the corner of the room, a failed attempt from his dad to get him into sports. It was a heavy proper bat that would definitely do the trick, and he'd rarely heard of anyone dying at the hands of a cricket bat. Perfect.

"And this definitely won't hurt her too much? And she won't remember a thing?" Ben worryingly, but full of excitement, asked the gravelly voice buried deep inside him.

*"Cross my heart and hope to die."*

That was good enough for Ben. Whenever he said that, he meant it, unless he had his fingers crossed behind his back. But Ben didn't think the demon voice had fingers, or a back, so he had to be telling the truth.

From the hallway, he could hear Carly on the phone chatting to one of her friends. Ben crept to her door and peered through the keyhole like he had so many times before. Dad wouldn't let them have locks on their doors, so he knew he could enter; he just he normally wasn't allowed.

*"You make the rules today,"* the voice reassured him. Ben nodded.

Carly had a shirt on, covering the top half of her body, but on the bottom half she only wore a pair of black knickers - ones that Ben had held to his nose a few times. It looked like she was in the process of getting changed when she took the call. Seeing her in this state only got Ben more excited as he admired her ass cheeks poking from the tiny underwear. He damn near creamed his boxers right there and then, but there was something bigger at stake tonight. He had to hold it in.

Ben waited for Carly to finish the call, and when she turned back to her wardrobe he quietly snuck inside with the bat raised high. While his room was painted blue with collectibles flung all over the place, his sister's room was yellow and piled high with clothes and makeup. Opposite the door she had a large freestanding mirror, and as Ben entered, he caught his reflection in the glass. He hadn't noticed up until now, but he appeared to have scars and scabs all over his face. *How long had they been there?* He caught himself staring at them for a moment too long, as Carly turned to spot him in the doorway holding the bat aloft with the weird decaying rot smudged across his face.

"What the fuck are you doing in my room, you freak?" she shouted, seeing him with what she thought was a mask and holding the bat like some fucking nasty ridiculous slasher.

Ben hadn't heard the dickweed come in; he'd been too caught up in the moment. He swung the bat that was still at his side at Brad, but the older boy avoided the swing and started shouting something about 'who was he,' and 'what had he done to Carly?' He looked fucking pissed and rocked Ben with a right hook that knocked him into the hallway with his trousers still around his ankles and cum still dripping from his semi. Ben could see the mirror through Carly's doorway and watched as the scars, scabs, and decay faded his face. Had Brad knocked them off? The voice was gone too. *How hard did Brad hit him?*

His eyes moved away from his reflection in the mirror to Carly crying on the floor, and it suddenly occurred to him that he'd caused that. Brad looked towards him, finally noticing it was Ben that had attacked Carly. He looked sick to the stomach and like he wanted to kill the little punk; instead Ben's lights went out as Brad knocked him the fuck out with an angry frustrated punch.

*

Ben's parents were mortified when they were called home and told about the attack. They'd always suspected that Ben was going to be some kind of sex pest... but RAPING his fucking sister! That was too much to handle for even their wild imaginations of what their perverted son might become. Ben told the officers that a voice inside his stomach told him to do it and mentioned the rot, something that Brad backed up, saying that Ben definitely had something going on with his face but couldn't exactly describe what.

It wasn't the first time this fucked-up face thing had been mentioned of late. The officers wondered if this was another one of those viral things that the dumb kids always took part in. The stupid shit that always resulted in someone dying in the end.

Planking while on a balcony, that kind of bullshit ... but the youngster insisted it was nothing like that.

His internet browser did not help his case one little bit. What fucking thirteen year old watches a woman fuck a horse and take a load of its spunk in her mouth? Not to mention the literal thousands of drawings of woman with their panties on display, including a whole notebook dedicated to a girl that looked remarkably like his older sister. No, this kid was a fucking serial killer waiting to happen. He'd already raped his God damn sister. But this stuff about the weird face was starting to get worrying. Someone needed to put a stop to the depraved trend right fucking now.

# Nathan Henwick

Nathan was a nervous wreck, and why wouldn't he be? It had taken him forever to pluck up the courage to ask Jack out on a date. There'd been months and months of staring at him from afar while dreaming about the little interactions they'd had. He'd relished the moments of them being together, even if it was only while buying clothes he didn't need from the shop Jack worked at, or 'accidentally' bumping into him in the outside world, *nothing to do with him practically stalking the guy*. His intentions were honourable though; he just had a crush. It wasn't like he was going to go all bunny boiler on him.

He'd brought so many T-shirts from the clothes store just to catch a glimpse of his would-be future husband behind the counter. So many times he'd had to hang back in the queue to make sure Jack served him, and no-one else. He'd tried to be subtle about it but one of the girls working there definitely clocked what he was up too. She didn't need to be a detective to figure out he was hoping to be served by Jack. Nathan wondered if Jack's colleague ever brought it up with him. *Was that something he could ask over dinner?* 'So Jack, did your co-worker tell you I was stalking you?' …Probably something better left to after they'd walked the aisle.

They'd decided on a restaurant for their first date after Nathan finally built up the courage to mention he had a thing for the hunky shop assistant. Despite the nervousness vibrating through his body now he was sitting in the restaurant, Nathan was massively relieved at the suggestion. He'd worried Jack would want to go to some loud club, or super trendy bar. That wasn't Nathan's scene, and while he'd go there for Jack, he was happy they'd chosen a restaurant where they could actually hear each other speak and get to know one another. Nathan was definitely more of a food and wine guy than loud music and a pint.

The awkward decision had needed to be made before making his way to the nice not too expensive not cheap too restaurant: whether to wear something he'd bought from Jack's store or not. Would it be a reminder of work? Or was he over-thinking it? He decided on a neutral shirt that wasn't from either the shop where Jack worked, or one of their nearby competitors. *He was definitely over-thinking it.*

They'd set the time for seven, but as always, Nathan arrived early. Their table was already available, so the waiter seated Nathan and brought him his first drink while he sat anxiously looking at the entrance, praying Jack would turn up. He hadn't doubted his appearance beforehand, but now, seated with everyone in the restaurant probably knowing he was waiting on someone, he worried Jack would no-show.

He didn't have to worry though. While Jack was five minutes late due to the taxi, he did show. Nathan couldn't help but admire Jack as he was escorted to their table. He'd come wearing a nice ironed crisp blue striped shirt and smart trousers, a far cry from how Nathan was used to seeing him in the shop. His charming hair was still as scruffy as ever and Nathan wouldn't have it any other way. Jack's thick muscular arms bulged under the shirt too, *that was going to be a distraction.* It was bad enough getting lost in his blue eyes, let alone thinking about those arms wrapped lovingly around him.

Nathan awkwardly stood to greet Jack upon arrival, which got a sincere smile from his date. *Did he find the gesture cute? Thank fuck.* Nathan asked him about his day a couple of times, nerves really kicking in, and Jack politely told him while then trying to steer the conversation towards Nathan. After all, Nathan knew far more about Jack than the other way round. Jack found out Nathan was an aspiring artist, mostly working within fine art. 'Pen and paper, not digital,' Nathan assured him, much to Jack's amusement. 'Of course,' he'd answered. Nathan looked the type that would do everything as old school and retro as possible. It was one of the things that attracted Jack to him.

They conversed more during their starters with the obvious getting to know you questions. Any siblings? Family? Likes? Dislikes? A little more about their jobs and current living situations. All small talk and all an absolute delight for Nathan, who'd been dreaming about this day for nearly a year. He'd made up so many stories in his head about who Jack was and what his life was like, getting them answered now was like a fun game. It took everything he had at times not to jump from his seat and shout 'I knew it.' He did have to be careful about remembering the reality from his own fantasy, but that wasn't too bad of a problem to have after all this time.

Jack had taken a fancy to Nathan after his co-worker Lisa told him the guy wanted him bad. 'Practically stalking you,' was the term she used. Jack wasn't sure if she meant that as a positive or negative, but Nathan was sweet so he went with positive. Jack hadn't noticed Nathan's affection until that point despite, as Lisa said, 'even a blind person could see it.' Recognising the signals wasn't Jack's strong point. He was fine once he knew; more than fine, in fact, as he was a very confident and easy-going guy. It was just those pesky initial tell-tale signs he was blind to.

Nathan couldn't believe how well the date was going. He was certain he'd fuck it up at some point, but so far so good. He'd even ordered himself a steak rather than a salad or some bullshit, as he didn't get out to restaurants much and wanted to take full advantage. They got a bottle of wine between them too, which was nice. It was red when Nathan would have much preferred white, but he didn't want to cause a fuss and Jack had mentioned earlier in their get to know you quiz that he preferred red.

*"You should have gotten white then, you pussy,"* a disturbing voice suggested. Nathan looked up, thinking the waiter had returned and made the comment, but that wouldn't have made sense. The waiter didn't know what he was thinking. Surely? Jack carried on talking about how therapeutic he found the gym while Nathan searched for the source of the unsettling voice. During the search, he managed to not only fail to work out where the hell the voice came from, and who it belonged to, but also completely missed everything Jack said. He had to just nod along like he was listening. Nathan really had wanted to pay attention to every single word. He wanted to memorise it all and play it back in his head over and over at home later, but that voice... it was so troubling. And rude. Sinister even. *And where the hell had it come from?*

"You ever go to the gym?" Jack asked, slightly frustrated as he noticed Nathan looking around the restaurant rather than in his direction. He wasn't needy or anything, but it was polite to look at your date when they're speaking.

"Huh?" Nathan replied trying to refocus on Jack's beautiful blue eyes rather than whatever the fuck that voice was.

"You ever try the gym?" Jack asked again with a curious smile as he tried to shake off the brief frustration. He wanted this to work. The smile shaped halfway between flirtatious and 'what the hell are you thinking about,' before he noticed something across Nathan's face. Was his skin peeling? Was that some kind of dry skin thing, or an infection? It looked to be slowly spreading, and darkening? Did Nathan know about it? Was that what was distracting him?

In truth it was pretty damn obvious Nathan had never been anywhere near a gym. He was as skinny as a rake with little to no build whatever. Noodle arms. Stamina wasn't his thing either. Nathan didn't mind walking, but if he could avoid it, he would.

*"Told you,"* the smug voice laughed. *"He thinks you're a fucking pussy, look at the way he's staring at you"*

"I'm not a pussy," Nathan abruptly said aloud to the voice while looking at Jack, unaware of the rot that had crept around his face. He could feel a slight itch, an irritating burn, but put that down to annoyance. Although he wasn't sure at who. Probably soon to be himself.

"Hey, whoa, that's not what I meant," Jack defensively replied. He'd been having a good time up until this point and didn't want to scare Nathan away. He could tell his date was nervous, but wasn't expecting that kind of reaction. He was hoping the question could lead to a little flirting, maybe some minor sexual innuendos. He hadn't considered the possibility of it being an insult.

The decay around Nathan's face grew. It stretched from his cheek and mouth towards his nose and up around his eyes. Jack swore he saw something wriggle under the skin, but that couldn't have been what he saw? Getting a little perturbed by the rot, Jack decided he needed to mention it. It felt rude bringing up someone's skin condition, but it was becoming distracting.

"Are you ok...?" he asked Nathan, gesturing towards his lower cheek and mouth, desperate not to offend his date further. Nathan didn't know what he meant, but the itch around his cheeks was growing stronger. The burning sensation felt more prominent too, albeit not in a painful way, which was strange in its own right. Nathan felt the bottom of his face and pulled his hand back quickly; the texture was all wrong. It felt soggy. His eyes instantly lit up, *what the fuck was happening?* He had a sudden urge to call for the cheque and get the fuck out of there asap.

Jack was beginning to think the same. This wasn't the first

time a date had turned sour for him, and while it would make a funny anecdote for his colleagues, he liked Nathan and had high hopes for the evening. But he didn't understand what was happening. Why Nathan had stopped listening to him like he was suddenly bored. Then there was the whole face thing. Jack didn't want to seem superficial, but fuck, that was some ugly skin thing going on there. The urge to kiss the nervous handsome stalker was fading fast.

The waiter brought their mains, breaking up the awkward silence that hung in the air after Jack mentioned Nathan's face. Steak for Nathan, and fish for Jack, who was quickly losing his appetite as he stared at Nathan's decay. The waiter gasped too as he caught a peek of the erosion. He hadn't meant to, and knew he was going to get a right telling off from his boss over it, but it caught him off guard. What the fuck was that? It looked like part of his face was beginning to fall off.

Nathan held his wine aloft and gawked at the rot himself in the circular reflection of the glass. *Shit.* His hand instinctively reached towards it again. The disgusting texture felt even worse this time, a stagnant wetness lay atop of the dry peeling blistered rot that used to be his face. Even more disturbing was both the waiter and Jack were watching him like he was some kind of oddity. Dinner and a freak show.

"I'll be back," Nathan tearfully stuttered as he raced towards the bathroom, leaving Jack a little perplexed and worried, and the waiter wondering what the hell he'd stumbled across.

*"Now he's definitely going to think you're a pussy"*

"Will you shut the fuck up with this pussy shit!" Nathan screamed as the voice laughed at him. Such a fucking condescending obnoxious laugh too, mocking him with ease. Like it knew the exact buttons to push and took glee in hammering them down. Nathan paced the bathroom, glad to be alone but also scared shitless at whatever the fuck was happening to his face. He took a quick glance towards the mirrors. The rot was still there, and still painless.

"What are you?" Nathan asked. looking away from the mirror; he'd already seen enough.

*"I'm you."*

"You're not. Am I going crazy?"

*"No, you're just being a pussy,"* the voice smirked. *Can a voice smirk?* Because that's exactly what it felt like it did to Nathan.

More tears started to spill from Nathan's eyes, but he couldn't feel the drops as the decay spread to his eye sockets and stifled the feeling. He wanted to scream too, but the erosion held his lips together like glue, stopping the sound from escaping. His face was being held prisoner.

"Please get this off my face," Nathan pleaded with the voice as it released its grasp on his mouth, happy it had asserted its dominance. "I want to finish my date," he whined.

Things had been going so well too, better than well. The way-too-soon dreams he'd been having of Jack being *his* man had begun to feel possible, despite his own self doubt. But now?

*"Oh it's already over. He's seen what a freak you are. How pathetic you are. What a fucking PUSSY you are. He's already on his phone hooking up with someone else."*

"No."

*"Of course he is. Why would he be interested in someone like you? You're nobody. You're invisible. This is a charity date at best,"* the voice sneered, with such conviction it was hard to deny, especially as Nathan's own anxiety agreed. *Or was that the voice agreeing?* He couldn't tell. The hellish voice deep inside Nathan knew it had him.

*The Rot's power was still limited. It had only just began its re-emergence. It was still figuring things out. The best approach. What it could and couldn't do. What it could get away with. When it needed to twist or encourage, manipulate or threaten, give or take. So many ways to get what it needed. So many possibilities. Yes, this was only the beginning, but it could already feel its power growing. Its will getting stronger. Its evil presence becoming more consuming, more vindictive. Nastier. Searing. Oh fuck this felt great. Addictive. Hook it to its veins, if it had any. The lives it could ruin were endless, and they needed to be. It had a long way to go yet. The power it could wield was overwhelming, but, one step at a time. It was unstoppable - well not yet, but soon it would be. But first, it had to gather more strength.*

The rot faded from Nathan's face, revealing his tearful eyes as he finally felt the little droplets running down his cheeks. No permanent damage too, which was a huge relief. Nathan thanked the voice for releasing him, but it didn't reply. *Maybe it was no longer there?* He headed to the sink and splashed cold water over his face, trying to work out what the fuck he would say to Jack, if he was still there. How on earth could he explain this, when he had no clue what *this* was? He couldn't just tell the truth because the truth was fucking insane. And on a first date? He wouldn't believe it himself. He'd think the person was taking the piss, so why would Jack think any differently?

He brushed his hair back with his hands and tried to smile to himself. It looked fake, but it was better than whatever smile he could manage with that fucked up rot spread across his mug. He knew the sensible solution was to tell Jack he was sick, go home, and cry himself to sleep. Tomorrow was a new day type deal. Then he could put whatever crazy hallucination that was behind him... *Although didn't Jack and the waiter both comment on the decay?* Fuck it, he'd waited too long for this moment. He needed to salvage the date and make sure he brought his A-game if there was a follow up, which he highly doubted there would be at this point. That was all the more reason to at least finish this one on some kind of high.

Nathan exited the toilet and breathed a sigh of relief seeing Jack was still there, and he hadn't touched his food. He'd waited for him, *bless*. He looked mildly annoyed, and perplexed, but that was understandable.

"You alright?" Jack asked as Nathan sat, his tone somewhere between concerned and frustrated.

*"Now show him you're not a fucking worthless pussy,"* the demonic grim voice suddenly instructed. as Nathan no longer felt like himself. Out of body wasn't quite the word for it, more trapped inner body. Whatever the fuck it was, he'd lost full control and went absolutely batshit crazy.

Nathan grabbed the steak knife from beside his plate and leapt across the table, plunging it deep into Jack's shoulder as he sent his date's fish toppling to the floor. The table flipped over. A second stab caught Jack in the chest, barely missing his vital organs, while a third diced his fucking ear off and sent blood spurting across the floor while the ear settled alongside the ruined fish. Jack, being the much bigger of the two, tried to throw Nathan off, and should've been able to with ease despite the stab wounds and blood lost, but Nathan was stronger than he looked. A lot stronger than he looked. Bordering on not possible.

Panic hit the restaurant as various patrons fled for the emergency exit while others shouted at Nathan to get off the poor guy. *Fuck him* Nathan thought; if he couldn't have Jack, no one could. *Why did he suddenly feel that way? Did he feel that way?* It didn't matter. This was happening. Nathan stabbed Jack several more times, like a man possessed before digging his fingers into the shoulder gash and trying to rip it the fuck open. He found purchase amidst the blood and gristle and tore the gap wider while Jack screamed in an agony he had no idea existed. Nathan grabbed a loose fork from the overturned table and poked inside the open wound, jabbing at a tendon like he was going to pull it out for a snack.

\* \* \*

Which is exactly what he fucking did.

Even in his trance-like state, it surprised Nathan when he popped the loose tendon in his mouth and began to chew, but he was soon back for more as he started digging into the muscle. Nathan then carved up Jack's chest some more with the steak knife before the rude waiter tried to heroically drag him off.

The waiter got a steak knife through the neck for his trouble, and earlier rudeness. That seemed to send a message to everyone else remaining in the room that wanted to be a knight in shining armour as the waiter collapsed to the floor in a fountain of blood. He was dead before his hands even tried to stop the spray. Everyone still inside the chaotic restaurant took a step back, heeding the warning. Not that many people were left, just the ones caught on the wrong side of the room and worried to cross Nathan. They fucking should be worried because they'd suffer the same fate if they fucking interrupted him again, Nathan thought as he chewed on *his* Jack's stomach meat.

Nathan dug the fork into Jack's gorgeous dead blue eyes that he'd admired for so long next, plucking them out and gobbling them up. He wasn't sure at the exact moment Jack stopped breathing, but it didn't affect the taste. The important thing was no one else could have him, and Nathan got to eat out at a nice restaurant. He didn't realise how hungry he was until he gnawed on Jack's lips, half giving him the kiss he'd always wanted to, and half eating the fucking things. *Best of both worlds.*

By the time the police tasered him, Nathan had devoured most of Jack's face and honestly, it tasted fucking amazing. All this time thinking about holding his hand, kissing him, touching him, and it turned out the most incredible sensation was fucking gorging on him. Whether that was Nathan's opinion, or the voice's, he was unsure, as it felt the two had briefly merged and become one. The electricity pulsing through his body put an end to that, or at least concluded their business together. Either way, Nathan was out cold while the voice and rot were gone.

*

The reports were weird and sketchy at best, with plenty of inconsistencies. 'Some kid apparently donned a possible mask and ate his date's face in the middle of a crowded restaurant while stabbing and killing his waiter in the process.'

All the witnesses confirmed the attack, but stories of the assault varied depending on view, and how quickly they got the fuck out of there. The CCTV showed the attack, but it made no sense, as there appeared to be no real provocation or motive. The kid had no priors, and was by all accounts a lovely human being. Shy, and a little awkward, but generous and kind. Then he's eating his date's face in the middle of a restaurant. Makes you wonder.

And the evil voice? The Rot? What was that about? Nathan had told the police afterwards that a voice was controlling him. That was some bullshit right there if the officer ever had heard, yet he wasn't the first person to mention this so-called rot and evil voice according to their system. No matter; he obviously wasn't the person everyone thought he was, and the nut-job cannibal would be locked up now surely never to see the light of day again. It was times like this the officer wished there was still some kind of death penalty, because this fruitcake was clearly beyond any kind of rehabilitation. Who the fuck eats people?

# Rachel Winters

Revenge! That's what the dark frightening voice in the bowels of her gut promised Rachel. Savage, hideous, wrathful, blood-soaked retribution ... and, fuck, did she want it. That voice knew exactly what button to press and slammed it down, jolting Rachel into life. She'd been lying in a hospital bed for nearly a week since the attack, which was the polite formal way of putting it. Brutal, reprehensible gang rape was a far more accurate description. She was due to be released later that day, as she was taking up a bed ... which, again. was worded differently and made to seem like she was fixed enough to be set free, but Rachel knew it was lack of beds and staff. Plus, fixed? What a fucking joke! She'd never be whole again after what those depraved animalistic cunts had done to her, but the voice promised she could make sure they would never do it again.

Rachel hadn't told the police who beat and raped her, but she knew. She'd seen their faces, recognised their voices; hell she'd served them the beer that helped fuel their rage on that darkest of nights. They'd been trying to get into her pants all evening at the pub, and when she wouldn't let them willingly, they took her unwillingly. Not only did all four of them hate fuck her, but they beat the ever-loving shit out of her as well. Left her looking deformed, such was the unrelenting force of their sick battering. And the icing on the cake, 'if you tell anyone, the same will happen to your sister.' They meant it too, and would probably find a way. *The sick fucks.* Who threatens to do that to a fourteen year old?

She'd spent the last week in agony, with her body destroyed and her face unrecognisable to the point where she didn't want any visitors. *What was to be said anyway?* The doctors and nurses assured Rachel her face would look better when the swelling finally succumbed, but there was significant damage to her cheek and orbital bones. Plus, 'look better' was a far cry from looking good. Back to normal. Fixed. No, Rachel was broken. She'd always be broken from now on. A part had been sadistically taken from her. She thought she'd spend the rest of her life as a victim, but fuck that shit. *'You can have your revenge. You can fucking tear them apart,'* it had told her. Sign her up. That dark evil voice soothed her damaged soul. Oh, they were going to fucking pay!

They would feel the repercussions of dragging her into the alley, of smashing her face against the unforgiving brick wall. She would show them unforgiving. She'd get her revenge for the punches to the face, for kicking her while she was down. She'd make them pay for tearing off her clothes and making jokes about how wet she was for them. That wetness was blood after the asshole called Deano broke her nose and blood gushed down the length of her naked exposed body. And if it wasn't the blood making her 'wet,' it was the tears as she begged and pleaded for her life. She honest to God thought they were going to kill her. They threatened to as well, like it was the funniest joke any of them had ever told.

Then Tyler mounted her like a dog in heat. Just jammed his mammoth cock deep inside like he fucking owned her. The pain almost distracted from the broken nose, but then Wayne stomped down on her stomach, breaking a couple of ribs, and Tyler instantly sprayed his 'nut butter' deep inside her. Two pumps and done after that stomach crunching stomp. He then told the others how he'd 'emptied his balls into her slutty cunt.' That's how they'd been talking all evening at the pub. She should have thrown them out earlier, or called the cops, but nights had been slow of late and they'd been buying plenty. A trade far from worth it in the end, but she was only trying to make some money and allow the lads room to blow off steam. They were regulars with long-suffering wives and girlfriends, kids at home waiting for Daddy to return. Not in a million years did she think they'd take things this far. But they had.

After Deano and Wayne had taken their turns 'riding' her, Bruce got leftovers. "What have you guys done to her pussy?" he quipped, sending the others into hysterics. Rachel didn't find it amusing. She was raw and bloody, and somehow still fucking conscious. Still remembering and documenting every detail as he defiled her once more. He'd taken the ass because there wasn't anything left of the pussy. *Charming*. And taken the ass he had. She still wasn't sure if she could walk properly a week on.

Then came the worse of all, the threat. 'If you rat on us your delicious baby sis gets it next, and we'll bring the whole fucking team,' they howled, referring to the Sunday league team they all played in. Rachel liked to think the rest of them couldn't be as evil as these cunts, but then she'd thought they were mostly harmless too before that night. Rough around the edges and not the sort of guy you take home to your parents, but surely not capable of this? Capable they were, and a hell of a lot more. They even beat on her some more after raping her, just for shits and giggles.

Walking away, they made jokes about whose rug rat it would be, as one of them had to have knocked her up. Bruce pleaded innocent; after all, he'd fucked her in the ass, not wanting their sloppy seconds… or fourths. Then he joked about how they probably killed the baby with the beating afterwards. 'Birth control,' he bellowed, to another round of hooting.

The week barely healed any wounds, and the mental scars only got worse. They wouldn't ever be getting better.

*"Oh but they could,"* the cunning voice interrupted, and it was right. No matter the manipulative undertone, whatever this voice was, it wasn't trying to lie to her. It had its own agenda, but it fit in with Rachel's needs, so who the fuck cared. She

couldn't be fixed, but vengeance was its own form of medicine.

The police had been angry at her for not naming the perpetrators. They suspected she knew and couldn't understand why Rachel wasn't naming names. They gave her the speech about how a lot of rape victims know their abusers but don't tell, and how that's a cycle that needs to stop. They didn't understand. It wasn't just the threat to her sister that stopped her informing the police, it was everything. They'd humiliated her. Broken her. Claimed her as their own. Hell, they might have even impregnated her. The sick fucks! She was still in shock over the whole ordeal and the police kept pressing her like it was a fucking job interview. The least she deserved was some time and space.

Now she was glad she hadn't told, hadn't 'ratted,' because fuck, were they going to pay.

"You want to rip them in half?" the devilish voice asked, although it was more a statement than a question. When she'd first heard the voice, she thought it was her own, but it wasn't; it was something else entirely. It had come with an itch, a slight burn to her already sore and destroyed face. She noticed some kind of rot and decay spread across the swelling, but it made no difference. Her face was already ruined. It wasn't her face anymore anyway. Plus, this rot felt powerful. Sinful. She could feel a change, and embraced it.

"Time to make them pay."

Rachel didn't bother to check herself out; she just threw on a coat and left. She could barely move at first; everything ached. But the Rot, as she somehow knew it was called, soon fixed that. It told her to forget the pain, and she did. It told her it had 'bestowed upon her a new strength.' That's how it talked, old-worldly, like it was some ancient evil. Rachel didn't care. The voice could belong to Satan himself, as long as it allowed her to take her revenge.

She knew the four assholes would be at the pub she worked
at. For starters, it was early afternoon and they always met for a
couple before heading home to their families. Secondary, they'd
be there because of the audacity of it. They wanted to be there
when she finally returned so they could smirk and joke, or
maybe even mock concern. Fucking cunts!

*"They deserve a gruesome death."*

Rachel nodded in agreement. Damn fucking right they did.

*

To say the lads were surprised to see Rachel so soon after the
shit-kicking they'd given her was an understatement. When she
walked through the pub door, only wearing a nightgown and a
jacket, with her legs and face still covered in bruises and
bandages everywhere they could be wrapped, it took everything
they had not to burst out laughing. What a fucking sight she
was. Derek, the elderly landlord, was full of sympathy despite
not once visiting her in hospital. He'd been too busy running the
pub by himself, he'd told her over the phone. She understood,
right? No she fucking didn't, but he wasn't the focus of her
anger, and she didn't want visitors anyway. *The act of trying
wouldn't have hurt though.*

But the four cunts suppressing their smirks, they one-
hundred percent were the focus of her wrath.

"Jesus Rachel, what the fuck happened to you?" Deano
asked, lingering on *fuck* like it was a private joke between them.
If she had a gun, she would have shot the asshole between the
eyes there and then. But she didn't have a gun. Instead, Rachel
marched past them to the bar and ordered a whisky.

"Should you be drinking?" Derek asked, stunned by her
appearance. She really did look an absolute state, especially with
the the added rot. If he'd asked for ID the picture definitely

wouldn't have matched up.

"Make it a double," she firmly told him. He nodded and let her know it was on the house. Least he could do. *And it was just that, the very fucking least.*

"You want me to call someone?" he asked in a caring tone that felt sincere. He may have made excuses not to visit her in the hospital, but he was still human, unlike the scumbags behind her.

Rachel shook her head. "Not just yet." She downed her drink. "Another." He poured her a second and doubled it up once more. This time she didn't drink it. Rachel took the drink and slowly walked towards her rapists like she was going to join them boozing the afternoon away.

They thought the same, even pulled a chair out for her. Maybe she'd enjoyed herself; *all sorts in the world.* She wasn't there to drink with them, though. Rachel asked the voice inside her whether it really had given her a little something extra. The need for retribution was boiling over as she stood leering at their self-congratulatory expressions. Such fucking assholes.

*"Find out,"* was its cruel unnerving answer, except it settled Rachel's nerves.

All four smiled at her, not a flicker of guilt or shame between them. How was that possible? No remorse, no regret. They all looked pleased as punch. *How?*

Their smiles soon dropped when the rot began to swirl around Rachel's face.

"What the fuck?"

Rachel took a gulp, then spat the remaining whisky over Tyler and pulled a lighter from her jacket pocket. He was up in flames before the other three knew what the fuck had happened. They were still trying to figure out what was going on with her face. Had they caused that too? *Oh shit, Tyler's on fire.*

Next she smashed Tyler's pint glass against the table and

dug the remaining shard into Deano's throat. His hands wrapped around the wound but the blood wouldn't stop. It sprayed from him like the fucking sprinkler system that should have gone off with the fire. Derek had meant to see to that.

Wayne jumped to his feet and took a swing at Rachel, connecting good. He swore he could feel another rib crack with the body blow. She stumbled backwards but didn't stay down for long. Instead she grabbed a chair and threw it at Wayne's head, while Bruce tried to extinguish the flames engulfing Tyler with his jacket. Derek ran for the fire extinguisher out back, but fuck if he could remember which one he needed. *Didn't they all have different uses, or colours, or something?*

Rachel tackled Wayne to the floor, surprised by her own strength as she pinned him down. *"Told you,"* the Rot stated, at the extra strength it had indeed gifted her.

Wayne was a little shocked himself. Had they 'changed her,' like some horror movie cliche? She didn't put up this sort of fight when they fucked her against the harsh alleyway pavement and beat the holy hell out of her. She rained punches down on his face after hooking his arms under her legs. He lay unprotected beneath her as she punched her knuckles raw and broke her hand across his face. His nose shattered and his forehead began to bleed. She reached for an unbroken glass on the table and tossed the remaining beer over his nose, stinging the wound. *If only she had a salt shaker.* It was a dick move, but nothing compared to what they done to her.

Rachel prised his pie-hole open and then jammed the pint glass in his mouth, slamming her broken hand against the bottom of the glass. It smashed against his teeth, filling his maw with tiny fragments and bigger shards. Rachel held his mouth closed and slapped his cheeks, making him involuntarily whirl the glass around inside his gob. Not done yet, she grabbed him by the ears and slammed his head repeatedly against the unforgiving pub floor.

*"Harder,"* the devilish voice inside her ordered, and she duly obeyed. She would have cracked Wayne's fucking skull in half if she could, but Bruce dragged her off, leaving Tyler to drop and roll ... while Deano lay dead on the floor, having bled out. He got off lightly.

Bruce threw her across the room and reached into his bag, which had been sitting on the floor. He pulled out a pair of brass knuckles that he kept in case some asshole started on him. *Oh the irony.* Well, it wasn't some asshole starting on him, it was the woman he and his buddies savagely raped. Rachel ducked his punch as the two neared each other and she ended up back alongside Wayne. Realising her position, she stamped down hard on the dickhead beneath her. Her foot connected with Wayne's face as he tried to spit the glass from his mouth. She didn't crack a rib like he'd done, but she was sure something much worse must have happened, as blood poured from his mouth by the gallon load and he began to choke and convulse.

"You cunt!" Bruce roared at her.

She could only smile. God this felt amazing. The moment the voice suggested revenge, it made something still remaining inside her tingle, but the feeling of actually taking it? Wow. And she wasn't done yet. Bruce strutted towards her, showing the brass knuckles wrapped in his hand as Rachel backed towards the bar. He thought he had her, but little did he know it was the other way round. Once he followed her behind the bar, Rachel pulled the cricket bat Derek kept behind the counter from its hiding place and swung for the hills. She connected with his jaw, stunning him and making him take a step back. She was on him before he could regain his bearings.

A second wild shot knocked him to the floor, where she then proceeded to smash the bottles sitting on the shelves and stuck to the optics above him. Broken glass and alcohol rained down before Rachel once again pulled out the trusty lighter.

"No!"

"Yes."

He barely got the words out before he too was set ablaze.

Derek had already belatedly used the last fire extinguisher on Tyler when he saw Bruce go up in flames too. *Did he even have another one?* He scurried outside the pub instead; fuck this, the insurance company could sort it out. He wasn't getting burnt alive. He'd left his mobile inside, so searched the street for a passerby to use theirs and phone all the emergency services.

The rot on Rachel's face retracted, but the voice still lingered deep inside her, encouraging her to go further. *"Remember what they did to you."* She didn't need reminding; she had a constant playback on loop in her mind.

As Bruce was an ass man, that's exactly where she jammed the broken bottle of vodka which had fallen by her feet. He was still on fire when she yanked his trousers down and crammed the jagged bottleneck up his asshole. It burnt her arm in the process and she almost caught on fire, but it was worth it. She left him melting with the glass still ripping at his torn anus.

Wayne had choked to death after the glass stomp, so, like Deano, he too had escaped any further punishment. Rachel hoped the voice would continue her vengeance in whatever hell it came from and where they'd surely go. The Rot just smiled, or at least gave her that impression. That left Tyler who lay a smouldering mess on the floor. His whole body was burnt, head to toe. His face was blackened with blisters and his skin peeled and dripped all over him. Any remaining rag of clothing had melted onto his body. His hair was gone and replaced by a scalp that looked ready to be ripped off.

*"Go ahead,"* the voice suggested, as this time the Rot did fade away.

Rachel could feel the change. Whatever possessed her was

gone, the extra power taken with it. Her whole body hurt again and she couldn't stand. She fell to the floor alongside the barely breathing smoking wreck that used to be Tyler, but probably couldn't be considered so anymore.

"Help me," he somehow mumbled, despite his mouth hanging from his crispy face.

*Haha. As if.* The evil presence inside her may have left, but the thirst for vengeance remained. She wondered if his oversized cock had survived the blaze. Peeling away the melted trousers from his charred body, she took a look. Sure enough, the big dick hadn't fallen off. That could be sorted.

Rachel stretched for another big shard of glass. Just holding the fucking thing cut into her fingers. *Had it done that before when she was possessed?* She looked at her hands and noticed they were absolutely cut to shreds, and she was burnt in places too. Fuck it. She held the giant cock in her bloodstained, singed hands and began to saw. It was already black and blistered, so didn't take much extra work to cut loose as Tyler screamed. Somehow all his nerves weren't quite fried yet; Rachel was thankful for that. He did, however, die the moment the dick was removed, like he couldn't live on without the filthy rape tool.

The police and fire service arrived moments later and dragged Rachel from the blazing bar that had fully caught alight by this point. The fireman couldn't save the place as the innards were gutted, but they did stop the whole building collapsing in on itself. They'd dragged the bodies out too, but for what purpose was a mystery to Rachel. They deserved to spend eternity on fire.

*

She confessed all to the police, but left out the part about the Rot. After all, like they had said, she wasn't a rat. Plus, the evil voice had done her a solid. What those assholes had taken from her would remain lost forever, and life in prison for four counts of murder effectively meant her life was over, but theirs was most definitely over. They'd never harm anyone ever again. She didn't have to live in fear of them repeat offending, or worse, abusing her younger sister the way they had her. If all things were fair, they'd now be stuck in whatever hell the Rot emerged from, living in purgatory being raped by a glass bottle. Fuck them, they deserved it.

*That pure hatred had imbued the Rot with all kinds of dark power, but it had also taken its toll. Giving her the extra strength to take her revenge was something the Rot wasn't quite up to the task of doing yet, and had left it drained. No matter. It felt great, and tomorrow was a new day.*

# Wendy James

Wendy had been standing on the edge of the fifteen story roof ledge for the best part of the night, looking outwards into the darkness with tears rolling down her cheeks. She thought weeks ago that she'd shed all the tears her eyes could manage, but there had been plenty more, an endless amount. From her position she could barely see the pavement below that would soon be the end of her, but she knew it was there. Waiting. Maybe not waiting with open arms, but definitely with certain death, and that's all Wendy required of the cold hard concrete.

She always knew her life would end like this. It had been whispering to her since birth, the persistent voice that told her life was just too damn fucking hard and cruel. It had been proven right time and time again. Still, she endured. Wendy had allowed herself to get her heart broken, tried having a career, friends, a community, but it all fell apart, it always did. Her husband had abandoned her; she always knew he would. *Did that make it a self-fulfilling prophecy? Or was she just a realist?* Her friends followed because they were his friends really, not hers. It didn't matter that he was the lying cheating scumbag; they stood by him. After all, that's what friends do.

Work quickly followed, kicking her to the curb. No employer needed someone who cried all the time and constantly stormed off, unable to handle the pressures. They could talk about mental health all they liked, but when it came to putting it into practice, that was a different story. She didn't have much left after that. Her husband and work, that was her life. Her sad pathetic life. She wanted more; fuck, she had tried. She'd put herself out there and gone way beyond the boundaries the state of her mind would allow, but ultimately she still ended up on this rooftop, knowing that once she saw the sun one last time, she'd be dead. It was always going to end this way.

Wendy had tried and failed to kill herself three times before. Once, when she was twelve, she'd taken a razor blade to her wrists in the bathroom, before her dad kicked the door down and got her to the hospital after tightly wrapping towels round her wrist. He cried the whole time, and her mum was in hysterics. Wendy couldn't even remember why she'd done it now. Couldn't recall a single reason, other than life had just gotten too much. The doctors warned of chemical imbalances, and maybe that was still the case. It didn't matter; she couldn't fight the good fight any longer.

The second time had been after her first real boyfriend broke up with her. She'd taken a fuck ton of pills and called her best friend at the time to say goodbye. In hindsight, that one was a cry for help. She didn't really want to die, just wanted people to acknowledge how unhappy she was ... and maybe get back at her former boyfriend. He visited her in the hospital and acted sweet enough, but it was obvious he didn't want to be there. Ironically, he ended up with her bestie a little while later, and that was the end of that. She was surprised she didn't kill herself there and then when she found out about the pair of them, but it happened during a rare good period in her life.

She'd discovered travel during that time and had backpacked through a bunch of cities in Europe. Taken the train from capital to capital and soaked in the culture. Her parents were worried about her being alone, but they needn't have: it was the one time she felt safe to be around herself. She ate different foods, visited different museums and landmarks, tried different drugs, kissed different boys, and even indulged in a couple of one night stands. European bingo card. Fuck, how she loved that period of her life. If she could have kept doing that forever, then maybe she wouldn't be standing on the rooftop ready to see how high she could fly before the concrete put an end to her journey.

But money had run out and adult life kicked in. Before she knew it, the day to day grind was dragging her back into a pit of despair. The third suicide attempt was another overdose attempt, but this one wasn't a cry for help. This one was her having enough of the daily routine. Of life being overwhelming and underwhelming at the same time. What was the fucking point? She'd seen and enjoyed the best it had to offer and now was playing the post game, and who the fuck wants to do that for any real length of time? *Why live to eighty if you're just killing time?*

She could have tried to save up and travelled again, but it wouldn't be the same; that had passed. Even after her interfering neighbour alerted the authorities, and once again she'd been 'saved,' the idea of trying to recapture the better periods of her life felt impossible. That's what a mixture of illness and life does to you, it breaks you. It undermines your decisions and exposes your weaknesses, while letting you know there's only one way to escape it. *You can run, but you can't hide,* Wendy thought, standing alone on the rooftop.

Flickers of sunrise entered Wendy's periphery as she stood on top of the ledge. Soon she'd be able to clearly see below, and wondered whether anyone would look up. Whether a passerby would witness her last flight. Hopefully she wouldn't traumatise them too much if they did. She didn't need that kind of guilt, although she supposed it wouldn't matter. Maybe if her husband saw her plight, she could die with a smile on her face, but did she really think that?

*"Or you could kill him instead of yourself?"*

The suggestive comment didn't sound like the same voice which constantly predicted her death. The voice she normally heard was a resigned and familiar one, a voice that knew she'd been dealt a bad hand. This voice sounded more gravelly, more intense and disturbed. It came from inside her, just like the other voice, but from a different place. She always imagined the suicide voice coming from her head, but this voice was from some place deeper. Some place buried in the pit of her stomach, maybe.

It sounded different too. The voice which reminded her how worthless she was. and how she'd never be able to make a go of life as it was just too difficult, was her own. It didn't come from her lips, but it was nevertheless hers. This voice was unrecognisable. Its tone was nasty, and pure evil radiated from every word. It was aggressive and pushy. A bad influence. Not that her own voice was sunshine and rainbows, but it felt more honest despite its forlorn nature. This new voice was manipulative, something Wendy picked up on straight away.

*"You're about to kill herself anyway, so why not indulge?"* the voice added, in an almost cheery manner, like it was a fantastic suggestion. It grew impatient waiting for Wendy to answer, but hid that from her.

"I'm not a murderer," she finally told the sinister presence as a matter of absolute fact. Wendy didn't have a violent bone in her body, something that was perceived as a weakness by the world. A lack of fight, some might suggest, but that would be unfair and wrong. She had plenty of fight. She'd fought every single day of her life to not do what she was about to do, but every fighter eventually has their time no matter their grit and determination. It was time to throw in the towel and give someone else a go. Not that Wendy was holding anyone back, but she felt like she was taking up space that others could use better.

*"He deserves pain."*

"No one deserves pain."

*"He's a lying cheating scumbag. A complete asshole. A fucking prick. A right cunt."*

"Agreed."

*"And he needs to have his fucking heart cut out, just like he did yours."*

The voice put forth a compelling argument, but Wendy didn't truly believe any of those things. She was upset with him. He had cheated on her, with his fucking secretary of all things, but cutting out his heart seemed a bit much. Also, despite the cliche and her anguish over the whole damn situation, the secretary, Janet, wasn't a terrible human being. She was a fucking *whore*, only, she wasn't really. It was just life kicking Wendy down again and making sure any notion of everlasting happiness was a fairy tale. They'd fallen in love, then he'd fallen out of love with her. Shit happens. Just too often for Wendy to tolerate any further.

She'd been friends with Janet, having seen the woman on a weekly basis whenever she visited Andrew at work. They'd even done lunch together a few times. But once again, her friend had run off with her supposed man. The circle of life. *If the same shit keeps happening to you, then surely you're the problem, right?* Did Wendy think that, or was the voice trying to invade her thoughts? Twist and mould her into whatever it needed her to be? In Wendy's own mind, without interference from the evil voice but still listening to the negative one that plagued her entire existence, if she was the problem then it gave her even more reason to remove herself from the equation.

*"Kill them both,"* the voice violently suggested, feeling like it was losing its faint grip on Wendy. It wasn't used to failure, but recent events had taken its toll. While its power rose, its strength still ebbed and flowed, and it could feel Wendy's lack of interest in its proposal.

Wendy shook her head as she watched the sun rise higher in the sky. It was still half stuck on the horizon but the morning rays started taking effect and the pavement below begun to illuminate. She gazed down at her soon-to-be final resting place, at least with a heart beat. Wendy guessed she'd be scooped up and laid to rest some place else by someone, but who she didn't know. Her only real family were her mum and dad and they'd both died in a car accident a few years back.

That should have been her fourth and final attempt right there, but the devastation was too much. She felt too numb and weak to do anything other than cry for months on end, and by the time she could do something about it, Andrew had entered her life. A doctor who fell for his grieving broken patient; maybe that should have been the first sign this wasn't a happily ever after story. Not that Wendy believed in such things to begin with.

He'd saved her though. Both in a professional manner, and in a life worth living one. Their romance had been magical to begin with, after dealing with the initial grieving, and then her scepticism of believing anyone could want her. He treated her with such warmth and delicacy just when she needed it the most. In return, she gave him her vulnerable heart.

*"Then he ripped it out."*

He breathed life into her ruined world. For a few years, he was her saviour.

*"Then he crushed you like you were nothing. Look at you now, about to kill yourself over that pig. It's pathetic. He should be the one dead, not you."*

She thought they could be happy together.

*"Never. He was using you. You were a conquest to him, nothing more."*

The nagging feeling inside her had suggested this couldn't last forever, but she went with the flow and got a few more happy years out of life. More than she'd expected.

*"Of torment. Of delaying the inevitable. Of being a pawn in his perverted game. How he and Janet laughed at your expense."*

Everything hadn't been all bad, and for that, Wendy was

grateful.

*"He was cheating on you the whole time. You know that, right? He had his filthy cock in every pussy that walked through the door. Just like you. You thought you were special; you were just the latest in a long line."*

She missed the affection, but nothing lasts forever.

She knew she should be angry at him, but, barring travelling in Europe, living with Andrew was the best time of her life, during her most difficult period as well. He wasn't a replacement for her loving, caring parents, but he was what she needed. Put in that context, she could almost persuade herself she was the one using him, but that wasn't true. It was a mutual agreement, a mutual love, at least for a while. He gave her some of the best years of her life, and she'd returned in kind. Tragic really that it ended the way it did, but she couldn't hold a grudge. She wasn't letting him off the hook for the cheating and scumbaggery, but more just accepting that truly nothing lasts.

*"Why the fuck aren't you listening to me?"* the disturbing voice raged. Suddenly its persuasive tone evaporated and was replaced by something more akin to anger. Not an anger that was firing her up to do something untoward, but an anger directed *at* her, like a petulant child not getting another snack before bedtime.

"I'm not killing anyone but myself," she calmly told the irate voice.

She could feel it trying to change her mind, trying to make her do more than simply throw herself off the rooftop. It needed her to let loose and cause destruction, but she wasn't going to allow it that.

Wendy also felt something lightly spreading across her face, but she paid that no attention too, just like she ignored the attempted manipulation from the devilish voice. The sensation of the rot spreading cheek to cheek and wrapping itself around her lips was disturbing, but she didn't so much as lift a finger towards it. She tried her best to not even let on she was aware of the itchy, burning deterioration. She suspected the disturbing presence knew this, but she wasn't going to give it the satisfaction. It was invading her last living moments and deserved none of her regard.

Instead, she focused on the beautiful sunrise. The light bouncing around and bringing life to a gorgeous morning. The smell of bakeries and springtime filling her lungs. She couldn't actually smell or see any of these things, with it being the edge of winter and no pastries anywhere in sight, but in her mind they were there. That's how she wanted to remember this morning. That's the image she wanted in her head when she leapt from the rooftop and painted the pavement beneath her. It was her life, and her death, so she could imagine and act upon it in her own terms.

While the cold bleak morning was a closer metaphor to the life she'd lived, Wendy didn't want that to define her. She wanted to remember the few good times she'd had, and the moments in her life when she felt alive. When life was possible. For that, spring worked a damn sight better than winter. But she wasn't going to hold on for another few months for the first flowers to bloom and the mornings to lighten. She wasn't going to wait for that warmer sun to make its presence known during the transition from winter to spring. She was done; it ended now. So, using her imagination for her perfect final morning seemed a fair compromise. Her life, her terms.

*"It's a fucking waste,"* the evil voice inside her told Wendy, and it didn't mean the waste of her life; it meant a waste of not fucking destroying a few people before she croaked. *That was the voice's problem, not hers.* It would have to wait for another unsuspecting victim, because it wasn't getting shit from this one. The voice reluctantly agreed, but didn't tell her so. Like Wendy

ignoring the decay and burning across her face, the Rot suspected she knew she'd defeated it , but it didn't let on. *Fuck her.*

With the sun up, Wendy readied to take her final breath and jump, but she had to wait a moment as a young couple strolled arm in arm down the street beneath her. Early risers, or still enjoying something that started the night before. It was a sweet image and one she hoped meant that the couple were about to live a better life than her. *Not on the Rot's watch.* It hadn't faded away just yet and took its opportunity, mustering the little power it wielded over Wendy

As the couple below walked nearer, Wendy leapt from the fifteen story rooftop ledge and flew for a brief moment before landing smack bang on the young couple and taking their lives with her own. Wendy made the almighty splat on the pavement she knew she would, but with the addition - thanks to the Rot - of breaking a couple of necks before the crimson and organs spread across the concrete.

*That will fucking teach the cunt for ignoring me,* the petty malevolent voice thought. It was a missed opportunity, indicating that its powers weren't up to speed and its will wasn't at its fullest, but all things considered, it killed the same amount of people it intended. Andrew and Janet had an unknowingly lucky escape. But in the the eyes of the Rot, death was death and suffering was suffering, so the young couple dead in the blink of an eye still helped the cause.

*

Wendy's death was considered suicide and plenty was unfortunately said about the selfish nature of taking two young lives with her own. Andrew couldn't bring himself to attend the funeral after hearing the news, which meant Wendy was buried alone next to her parents with no one else knowing about her death, or being close enough to feel they had to say their final goodbyes.

# Stuart Wright

Stuart's rage had been building, bubbling, damn near boiling over long before the sinister voice uttered a single syllable. The voice wasn't even sure if it had influenced Stuart's decision to attack the staff and shoppers at the Happy Mart. It doubted it. It just sat back and watched in admiration as Stuart let loose and fucked up anyone and everyone in his path. The chaos was beautiful. The Rot could feel the hatred and anger. It could sense the darkness spilling over with every drop of blood that hit the grimy supermarket floor and with every shout, grunt, and curse that escaped Stuart as his rampage continued. The scared shoppers flooded towards the exits, but there were enough of them left inside for Stuart to fulfill the Rot's needs.

If Stuart had a gun, half the fucking shop would be dead already, but as he only had his own bare hands, the corpses piled up at a slower rate. Months of anger, frustration, and built-up hatred burst out of him in a single moment. The bottle of his rage erupted and the lid couldn't be replaced. The seal was broken. The first guy to catch Stuart's wrath was the person who, in Stuart's mind, caused the outburst, but it wasn't the crisp shopper's fault.

It was Stuart's former employer who'd fired him, and his ex-wife who'd left him. It was his fucking kids who wouldn't talk to him anymore. It was all the assholes and cunts online that whined all day about their insignificant problems. It was the lies and deceit spread on a daily basis. It was the whole fucking shitty world that had come down hard on him these last few years and left him a ruined man full of resentment and vices. But for Stuart, at this precise moment, it was definitely that crisp stealing motherfucker.

The bastard had grabbed the last bag of pickle onion Monster Munch practically out of Stuart's hand, then had the nerve to tell him go fuck himself when Stuart tried to snatch them back. The crisp stealer was built like a rhino, shoulders wider than Stuart's body, but a kick in the dick and a palm to the nose takes down just about anyone. What Stuart lacked in size, he made up for in unfiltered intensity ... which made have also been the cause of a few of his problems to begin with, but you can't help who you are. The son of a bitch at work could have listened to Stuart's side of the story rather than believing the douchebag he fucked up. His wife could have just shut the hell up for once and quit nagging him over every fucking single thing; maybe then he wouldn't have had to bust her nose.

His obnoxious bratty kids could have given their old man a break; they knew what their mum was like, a fucking dog with a bone. They'd had plenty of screaming matches with her down the years, but he was deemed to have gone too far. The rest of the family felt the same. Even his own mum sided with his now ex-wife Pauline over him. And fuck me, was that divorce quick; couldn't anyone see she'd been planning it? Was one-hundred percent premeditated, not far of entrapment. She'd goaded him into slapping her around. He wasn't proud of what he done; it had been in the heat of the moment, but he still believed the bitch deserved it. He especially believed it any time he'd had few beers; that's when it was crystal clear the cunt needed a slap.

Stuart was on his fourteenth beer when he'd headed to the Happy Mart to pick up another twelve pack and some much needed munchies. He'd snorted some shit too, but that was earlier in the day and had started to wear off. So why the fuck that oversized bastard decided to pick a fight with him over a bag of crisps was anyone's guess, But he wouldn't be picking any more fights. The low blow and broken nose had just been for starters; afterwards Stuart repeatedly bashed his fucking skull again the stained tiled floor and threw a bunch of crisp bags over him. The former caused ninety-nine-point-nine percent of the damage.

The Rot manifested moments before the swift kick to the big dude's balls. It wondered whether it had short-circuited Stuart upon arrival, but just got lucky. No manipulation required here; the guy was already unleashing. The Rot could give him an extra shove, but so far it hadn't been required. It watched on through Stuart's eyes as he slammed the guy's face down over and over. Stuart caught a glimpse of the rot which had began spreading across his face in the reflection of the now dead man's eyes, but paid it no mind. The kill felt good, like a release, that's all that mattered. *Next please.*

He stalked towards the assholes at the cheese-counter who, moments before the crisp incident, had refused to serve him while he slurred his words and kept pointing at an empty cheese stand. They couldn't magic up a batch no matter how hard he pointed, but Stuart wasn't accepting that shitty excuse. Stuart leapt the counter and nutted the first of the two employees. The guy went down like a sack of shit. *Fucking pussy.* The second guy, the one who'd refused to serve Stuart, or maybe just couldn't understand what he was trying to say - didn't matter now - backed off. Stuart quickly closed him down.

Before the helpless guy could even plead for his life, Stuart stuffed his fingers under the cheese wire and brought it down. The cheese man screamed as four of his fingers were effortlessly sliced off by the razor sharp wire with only his little pinky escaping Stuart's towering rage. Blood pissed from the diced nubs, spraying the remaining cheeses, much to Stuart's howling delight. He then put the fucker through the glass front of the cheese display counter and slit his throat with a loose shard because fuck that guy. Just another cunt standing in Stuart's way and looking down on him. Not anymore.

The meat man in the butcher section by the cheese was

Stuart's next victim. He came at Stuart with a carving knife he'd been using to cut turkey slices for a young family before the mayhem. Stuart easily disarmed the guy after his wild panicked swing and jabbed the knife he'd taken into the butcher's gut. He then proceeded to carve out a square while other shoppers watched in horror and reached for their phones either to call for help or upload the incident onto YouTube. As they tried to escape Stuart, they found crisp man dead with half his face missing in aisle four. "Clean up in aisle four," Stuart slurred over the tannoy system, much to his own amusement as he watched their discovery. He tossed the cut of the butcher's stomach into the ham display as he continued his maniacal laugh.

Stuart grabbed a bunch of knives around the meat section and started beaming them at anyone he could see, catching a few shoppers in the back as they tried to run. Jumping back over the counter, he booted an old lady who'd witnessed the murders in the face. She was too fragile to run and hit the ground hard upon impact, causing her head to crack against the tiles and her brain to swell. Stuart stomped further down the aisles towards the alcohol he'd initially come in for, muttering to himself about how *'they all deserved this.'* How it *'wasn't so funny stepping on him now.'*

Two would-be heroes tried to stand their ground, but while Stuart's speech was sloppy, his fighting wasn't. Stuart punched one guy across the jaw, right on the button, then head-butted the other. Both got in their own punches first, but Stuart walked through them like he was playing with a toddler, or an overactive kitten. He stomped down hard on broken-jaw's head, and smashed a wine bottle against head-butted's face. Neither man survived the evening as Stuart continued the feral assault, leaving them both as blood smears.

*God it felt fucking good to let the fury spill out.* He'd been holding it all inside for so long, too long; it wasn't healthy. He'd wanted to wrap his hands around his boss's scrawny throat for the best part of a year, but hadn't. The need to try and keep his job overtook his desire to strangle the cunt to death. In hindsight, the responsible choice hadn't helped him in the slightest, as he lost his job anyway and hadn't been able to get another since, while that asswipe continued to walk the earth. He should have fucking annihilated him.

Punching his wife in the face had been a lapse, a moment of unbridled violence that he hadn't kept inside, but looking back on it now he considered maybe he shouldn't have stopped there. After all, the bitch left him and took what little he owned with her while also poisoning his kids against him. He should have snapped that slut in two and taught the fucking kids a lesson as well.

He'd tried to somewhat refrain online with the ridiculous arguments and name calling and fucking non-stop complaining he witnessed on a daily basis, but again, it would have been much more freeing if he'd told them all exactly what he thought. He didn't want to be another asshole arguing online, but if he'd known how good the release felt he would have gone to town on the snowflakes and Nazis alike. Stuart didn't take sides, other than his own. The sides, as far as he was concerned, were him against the world; he hated every motherfucker equally. It felt like everyone had taken a shot at him this past year, so he wanted his pound of flesh back from all types. Discrimination be damned; he wanted to fuck everyone up.

When he reached the beer, another group of men confronted him. They'd all been sensible enough to grab a bottle from the shelf to use as weapons, but not sensible enough to stay out of the lunatic's way.

"You cunts got a problem," Stuart aggressively spat at the four, who were already doubting their stand. His face was practically falling off with the decay at this point, and all four guys could see it. The bottom of his jaw was red raw, his nose looked bent or rippling or something out of the ordinary. His eyes were half glazed over, while also staring at them. It was an unsettling fucked-up sight. The rot had spread across his forehead and back to his scabbed ears. The dry peeled skin flapped and was ready to drip off his face as he shouted and snarled at them. He looked more mutant than man, like he'd been dumped in a vat of toxic waste and let loose on the world. Whatever form the rot normally took, it was working overtime here.

All four took a step back, thinking Stuart was rabid. *Did rabies cause this?* They clutched the glass bottles tighter but none wanted to make the first move. They weren't sure whether whatever caused the rot and ultra-violent outburst was contagious or not. They'd initially thought he was drunk, and possibly off his fucking nut, but up close it was obvious something more drastic was going on. The only one not concerned about the state of his decaying face and mind was Stuart, he was more interested in gearing up for the next ruck.

"Come on then, you fucking pussies."

They collectively took another step back as Stuart strutted towards them.

"You need to calm down," one of the four nervously stated, seeing the bodies of the two men Stuart had just killed laying in a pool of blood a few aisles back. They looked positively fucked up beyond all possibility for the short amount of time he'd confronted them. He really was rabid.

"No one else needs to get hurt," another of the four tried explaining. The guy looked like a fucking accountant with his smart clothes and stupid glasses. The type of fuck who'd been talking down to Stuart his whole God damn miserable life. He'd make sure to kill that one first.

The voice wanted to say something; it wanted to intervene

and encourage Stuart to continue his rampage, but it didn't need to. Stuart's blood was still boiling. The hatred was still all too easy to see in his eyes despite the effects of the decay. Stuart had gone to a place he wasn't coming back from. Had seen red, and fully embraced it. All the fiendish voice had to do was sit back, enjoy the show, and lap up the hatred and violence. It wasn't used to being a bystander, but its services currently weren't required.

The toughest looking of the four men was next to speak, telling Stuart to put the bottle down. Stuart didn't even remember picking up a bottle, but he wasn't putting it down for that asshole. As the fourth stepped cautiously towards Stuart, gesturing for calm, Stuart attacked. He cracked the bottle in his hand over the accountant's head first before slamming an elbow into the nose of the wannabe tough guy. He smashed his fists repeatedly into the face of the fourth guy, who stayed up longer than Stuart thought he would.

The initial guy who told him to calm down was anything but calm as he whacked the back of Stuart's head with a cheap bottle of cider. Stuart absorbed the blow even as a second swing broke the bottle over his decay-ridden face. Stuart grinned at the fucker, letting him know he was dead for that, and there was absolutely nothing he could do about it. The guy tried to escape but slipped on the very cider that he spilt to the floor when smashing the bottle over Stuart. *How do you like those apples?*

Stuart stamped down hard on his downed opponent's leg, possibly breaking his shin. Next he jumped on the guy's right knee, bringing all his weight down on it and hearing a horrendously satisfying crack. He turned away from his latest victim back to the accountant, who lay in a daze on the ground. Stuart punted him in the face and gut several times over. He then grabbed a handful of bottles from the shelf and chucked each and every one of them at the accountant. They all smashed on impact, cutting the possible accountant's face and body, but Stuart wasn't finished with him yet.

He grabbed the accountant by the legs and dragged him through the pile of broken glass several times over before stamping down on his head, causing it it splatter into the already bloody and unforgiving glass shards. The stomp had gleefully become Stuart's go to finishing move. Next he picked up the tough guy and ran him into the end of the aisle. His face squished against the solid end-cap repeatedly, getting more squashed every time. After the fourth slam, his remaining teeth pieced his lips and his already broken nose practically fell off, while his eyes swelled shut and his skull cracked like a fucking egg. A bunch more vicious collisions put a permanent end to his pain.

Stuart had always been intense, and always believed himself to be a strong and capable fighter, but he felt on fucking fire today. Like he was juiced up to his eyeballs. He could tell something was different. He felt fucking berserk, such was the power and strength running through him. His face was burning, but a good burn, although when he touched it, it felt wet. He assumed it was from the copious amounts of blood he'd spilt rather than anything more unexplainable. He remembered seeing something on his face after the first kill but dismissed it as backwash from the splatter factor; parts of the crisp stealer must have flown onto him after he bashed his fucking face to mush. Stuart's deliberation of the mess on his face, and extra strength he seemed to possess, didn't last long as he remembered the other two fuck-heads that tried to put a stop to his fun.

Sirens blared in the distance but Stuart was way beyond giving a fuck. This was his final stand and he knew it. He wasn't going to jail again; been there, done that. He might not have the T-shirt, but thought, despite it being twenty-five years ago he probably still had the criminal record. Certainly felt that way on the recent job hunt. What's the point in rehabilitation when no-one was prepared to give him a chance? *Oh well.* He still had time to cause more damage before his time was up.

As he approached the last two guys, he saw a woman in her early forties cowering in the next aisle with her hands over her ears, like not hearing his destruction would make her invisible. *Well, she fucking wasn't.* Stuart smirked and made a beeline for her, briefly forgetting about the two remaining guys and his beer. She was pretty despite the tears, and had long brown hair like his cunt of an ex-wife. She was dressed in a similar fashion too. It didn't take much for Stuart's deranged mind to imagine it being her. It was impossible with Pauline moving to the other end of the country to get away from him, but here she was nevertheless.

He kicked her straight in the fucking head before she even looked up at him. Just a full on punt that sounded as sickening as it looked. Somehow, her neck didn't break on impact, despite the kick lifting her off the floor and rocking her head back as she crashed down. That was going to be enough for her until a sinister voice deep inside Stuart whispered to him.

*"Come on, you know you want do more than that."* Stuart paid no attention to the fact that the voice wasn't his; all that mattered was the voice was one-hundred percent correct.

It had been a while since Stuart had fucked a woman. His wife was the last willing one, although she wasn't exactly that willing half the time. He'd fucked a few hookers since, but because he'd been 'too rough,' none of them seemed available anymore. He'd even had a pimp tell him to chill out. A fucking pimp! Like they should be giving morality lessons. He was sure they'd slapped the filthy whores around way more than he did. Either way, he was cut off. But this wifey-looking bitch on the floor, he could do whatever he wanted with her.

The fourth guy, who'd endured the melee of punches, was back to his feet and rounding the walkway to meet Stuart. He stood in front of the fallen woman with his fists raised like he was ready for round two. Stuart once again wished he had a fucking gun; he'd end that prick instantly. Instead he bounded forward and tackled the guy to the floor before pounding his fucking face until he was hitting nothing but tile. The would-be saviour was paste. Stuart spat on the near-headless corpse as he got back to his feet. *Now where was I?*

The wife lookalike hazily crawled away from Stuart, but hadn't got far. The hard landing resulted in another bleeding head wound that left a telling trail. Stuart was sure there was some joke about cracked eggs with the amount of skulls he'd opened up in a supermarket but he was in too much of a frenzy for puns. Instead, he followed the trail around the corner where he was ambushed by the remaining guy from the four friends.

He assumed they were friends; maybe they'd just gathered together to take him down. *Well that fucking failed.* The remaining guy was no match as Stuart kneed him in the gut, and then slammed a second knee to his face when he doubled over. The guy slumped against the end-cap beside the other dead schmuck and Stuart proceeded to lay more knees in. Knee after knee crumbled his face before his breaths halted. Fuck all of them.

Stuart's evil grin returned to the escapee as she continued her slow, agonising crawl away. He got as far as ripping her clothes off and pulling down his own jeans before the cops stormed the blood-soaked supermarket. They rushed him as he mounted her. Stuart crammed his cock inside the traumatised woman and swung his fists at the police as they tried to apprehend him. It took eight of them to drag him off as he continued to try and plough her. Enraged that he hadn't cum before they pulled him off, he continued to fight the cops.

He fought through pepper spray and being tasered as the cops descended on the half-naked madman. He finally did cum when he snapped the neck of a young officer. *That felt better than even being inside the bitch.* After that the cops weren't trying to restrain him anymore. They beat the holy-fuck out of him. Their truncheons whaled down hard on Stuart over and over, with every shot determined to break his bones. All seven of them were in a fit of rage, having seen their young colleague's life taken before their eyes. They wanted blood. Two of them had cum stains on their trousers as Stuart had let fly during the neck break, while all the others had blood, now mostly Stuart's.

When they finally tired of hitting him, he was long dead. They all knew what they'd done wouldn't be considered the correct course of action, but fuck him. He'd killed multiple people, including one of their own. No-one would side with this asshole, and he wasn't alive to plead his case anyway. The Rot had remained through-out the whole attack, absorbing all the hatred and unflinching fury. The added bonus of police brutality had been a welcome surprise. A good day all round for the Rot, despite expending little to no energy.

*

The papers claimed Stuart was on pretty much every drug known to man and had rabies or some bullshit. It was all very mixed and contradicting, but they made it sound like he was on the bender of all benders and had gone completely fucking batshit crazy. Anyone left who'd witnessed the atrocity certainly attested to that. His toxicity report gave the claim some validation, but not to the degree being reported.

Others questioned whether this was related to the recent spate of extreme violence that was starting to grip the country. There were reports of his face looking rotten, but after the beatdown it was hard to tell what damage there had been beforehand compared to after. One of the officers thought he'd seen the decay but couldn't be sure, and the rest didn't care. The woman Stuart raped had kept her eyes closed during the entire attack and couldn't remember much after the bloodcurdling punt anyway.

Stuart was thrown in the furnace with no-one spilling tears for his demise, including his kids and ex-wife. The world was a better place without the piece of shit, they'd said. The dark voice that was the one true witness to the whole event would have begged to differ; it enjoyed its time with Stuart.

# Joe Sulley

Who the hell goes on a caravan holiday in the middle of November… in England? It was fucking freezing. Joe Sulley, or Grandpa Joe as he was affectionately known by his grandkids, was not enjoying his holiday one little bit. He loved his daughter, and three grandchildren, but he should have remained firm on his initial no. *No* I don't want to spend a week with you, your husband, and the kids in a metal tin can in the middle of nowhere in the winter. The metal tin can was fancier than the ones he remembered from his own childhood holidays, and nicer than the one he and his late wife stayed in back in the day, but still.

His daughter Sarah had talked him around like she always did. She had him wrapped around her little finger since birth. Sarah told him how much the kids would love to have their grandpa around, how it would be good for him to get out of the house. How Mum would have wanted him to enjoy some quality time with his family. All very manipulative, but not entirely wrong. Since April died, Joe had barely left their home. Forty-five years was a long time to be with someone, and she was taken too early. Cancer, just months after retirement. It could be a cruel world, yet Joe had learnt how this was a common story. *Why the hell hadn't they been told that while working non-stop towards retirement?*

He sat back on the living room sofa, or what qualified as a living room sofa in the caravan, thinking about the life they'd planned after retirement. The holidays they'd intended to go on were a damn sight nicer than this. They'd planned various cruises covering half the globe and knew they'd enjoy every single moment of it; they'd earned it. Neither had ever been on a cruise before, so it was something new they'd embark on together. Joe couldn't face the idea of a cruise now though; it wouldn't feel right. Without April it meant nothing, despite her making him promise he'd see the world for both of them. She *was* Joe's world.

Sarah, and her husband Mike, who Joe wasn't a big fan of but who April liked so he cut the guy some slack, were out spending some time together, leaving Grandpa Joe with the kids for an hour or two. He knew it would happen at some point on the holiday but fortunately wasn't the reason they'd brought him along. He didn't need to tell his daughter he wasn't a glorified babysitter because she already knew that. They'd raised a beautiful kind child who'd grown into a lovely responsible woman who never took advantage of anyone.

Why she needed three kids though, Joe wasn't sure. Maybe they were at fault for her being an only child. She'd always wanted a big family and began to fulfill that need the moment she'd settled down. A fourth kid was on the way, but the three she had didn't know that yet as it was early days. April would never get to know this one, barely got a chance to say 'hi' to the youngest before she passed. Joe couldn't help but shed several tears thinking about it. He wasn't an emotional guy, but thoughts of his wife missing out on the things she should be enjoying always upset him.

Seagulls slammed on the roof, breaking Joe from his nostalgic thoughts. They'd been doing that since he arrived, fucking flying rats. Constantly banging on the tin roof day and night, squawking away like they'd paid the fee for the week. They fought and argued more than the kids. The holiday had been cheap by British holidaying standards, but only because it was so far out of season that no one would have turned up otherwise. Joe always assumed these places closed in the winter months, but knew what they said about assumptions. So it was basically just Joe, his family, and a fuck ton of noisy seagulls. He'd seen a few other holiday makers dotted around the park, but everyone seemed to stick to themselves. The facilities were all mostly closed as well, meaning it was pretty boring for the kids, but they made their own fun.

Hayley was the oldest of the three girls at twelve. She was grown up for her age, but Joe thought all kids were now. The way she spoke and acted was nothing like how his Sarah behaved at her age, despite Hayley being the spitting image of his daughter. That wasn't to say Hayley was a horrible little thing; just, to Joe, kids really were a lot different now. Hayley always had her face buried in her phone and used ridiculous words Joe didn't understand. She did stupid fucking dances for her phone too, which Joe also didn't get. It had been sweet watching her dance as a little innocent girl, but these weren't those type of dances. It seemed inappropriate to Joe, but what did he know? Sarah assured him it was fine and that all kids behaved like that now.

Kate was the middle child. The ten year old had been a lovely kid but then turned into a right bitch. The way she spoke and acted had nothing to do with kids nowadays; she was a spiteful brat, and the one time Joe told her so Sarah scolded him for a week. It was soon after April died, so they put his words down to grief, but he'd meant it. He loved the kid - she was his grandkid after all, and was such a sweet little bundle of energy when she was a toddler - but something had gone horribly wrong somewhere down the road. Joe could pinpoint the exact location; it was when the youngest, Amy, came along.

Amy was three and finding her own voice and identity. She'd picked everything up quicker than her sisters, probably because she had them as examples. She learned to crawl quicker, walk sooner, and talked at a much earlier age ... to the point of now never shutting up. *Cute little chatterbox.* She was going to be a clever one, as long as she didn't keep falling for Kate's pranks and teasing. Amy followed her sisters around like a lost puppy, but they were both of an age where they didn't want to hang out with a 'baby.' That caused many tears.

Currently, Amy was wandering around the small caravan with a blindfold on, trying to find her sisters, who were hiding. Amy wanted to play hide and seek but the caravan was too small, so they'd talked her into doing it blindfolded. She'd spent the last five minutes not standing a chance of finding her sisters, as they quietly followed behind her doing their absolute best not to laugh. *Maybe Amy wasn't as clever as Joe thought?* The two older sisters kept making hush gestures to Grandpa Joe whenever he went to say something, so he kept quiet until Amy grabbed hold of his knee.

"Found you," she excitedly announced, lifting her blindfold. Her little face dropped as she realised it was Grandpa Joe and not her sisters - who'd both quickly ducked for cover. While Hayley was the spitting image of her mum, Amy had the same impossible to ignore grumpy face that Sarah used to use get all the biscuits and sweets she ever wanted. It melted Joe, but not the dark twisted voice that had infected him. Not the voice persuading him what horribly fucks these little brats were. The ominous voice telling Joe he should be on a big cruise ship with his loving caring beautiful wife, not babysitting a bunch of annoying fuckrats in a cheap tin can in the middle of fucking winter while his whore daughter was off gallivanting with that dipshit son-in-law. Joe might fall for Amy's adorable grumpy face, but the Rot didn't.

"What's wrong with you face?" Amy asked her loving grandad in her cute voice, while her sisters stayed ducked out of sight.

"Nothing," he replied, thinking she meant a concerned look. He hadn't noticed the decay spreading across his mouth and splitting apart his cheeks. He could feel some kind of itch but had been too deep in thought to pay the peeling of his skin any attention. Most of the rot was hidden by his still intact, but out of control, facial hair. Something he'd significantly grown since April's death. If more of his actual face was on display, the little shit would have probably burst into tears and run and hid from the 'monster.' She wasn't far off doing that now; sensitive kid, just like the other two used to be.

"How about Grandpa plays hide and seek with you all instead? Would you like that?"

Amy's little face lit up, momentarily forgetting the rot spreading towards his kind eyes. She loved playing games with Grandpa Joe.

"Go tell your sisters to hide while I count to fifty."

Amy didn't need asking twice. Her tiny legs bolted at top speed, barely avoiding the kitchen counter as she yelled for Hayley and Kate to hide, as Grandpa Joe was going to seek them. Sweet kid.

*"Wonder if her blood is as sweet?"* a voice deep inside Joe questioned. He wondered that too, but first things first.

"One... Two... Three..." he started shouting in his gruff voice.

While he counted, Joe considered all the things he could do to the girls. The voice kept reminding him of all the times they'd taken advantage of him, of how insensitive Kate had constantly been after April's death. How she tried to make it all about her despite Joe and Sarah's obvious grief. How Hayley was constantly mocking him about how little he knew about things nowadays. *The world didn't fucking start when you were born, young lady,* he wanted to scream at her, but hadn't. The Rot infecting the deepest depths of his soul made it abundantly fucking clear that he should have. *Who do these wretched brats think they are?* None of them would exist without Joe. None would be living the life they had if he hadn't raised their kind mother in a loving caring environment. Their kind mother who left him with the shitbags while she could wander off and fuck that bellend Mike. He knew damn well what time alone meant; it meant that poor excuse for a human could violate his little girl.

"Eleven... Twelve... Thirteen..."

He could bash that fucking phone over Hayley's head, see how see liked that dance. *Ha,* he laughed, despite the joke not working. Maybe he'd make her eat the fucking thing. Cram it down her throat and break those perfect white teeth she was so proud of. Maybe he'd break her teeth and scalp her, then force her to dance for the phone like she loved to do. He could watch the tears pour down her fucked-up newly ugly face before making an appearance at the end and breaking her spindly neck. Would that get him likes? Would that trend? Go viral? Fucking condescending slut with her stupid buzz words. *Kids nowadays.*

"Nineteen... Twenty... Twenty-one..."

He knew Kate would get it the worst because, if he was truly honest with himself, he hated that cunt. *Should have got the coat hanger out for that one.* He knew what was best for his daughter, and giving birth to that hell spawn was not best. Worst decision of her life, beside marrying that fucktard Mike. Joe saw how often Kate rolled her eyes at him. How she'd do impressions of him like he wasn't there. She never used to. Once upon a time, she was the sweetest little thing, Grandpa's favourite, but then she turned. Now she was like the kid from the *Exorcist.* Worse, she was the *Bad Seed,* that was it. Rhoda Penmark, that's who the bitch reminded Joe of. If that was the case, it was his duty to destroy the nasty little trouble maker before she seriously hurt someone.

*"Before she hurts your daughter,"* the demonic voice interrupted.

"Twenty-seven... Twenty-eight... Twenty-nine..."

She'd pay for her vindictive ways. Maybe he'd smash her head against the kitchen side? Although, it looked a little flimsy; cheap fucking box. He could put her through one of the dividing walls, but again, he doubted that would hurt. She'd be hiding in the bathroom with the door locked so he couldn't 'seek' her, so maybe he'd use something in there. Waterboard the bitch in the toilet. Maybe take a piss or shit on her while he did. 'Grandpa, that's disgusting,' she'd moan in her fucking whining voice while rolling her eyes at him and doing an impression. He needed to put an end to that voice, and the rest of her. Slice her windpipe with the smashed bathroom mirror after cracking her head against it. Watch her bleed out. *God that would be so satisfying.*

"Thirty-five... Thirty-six.... Thirty-seven..."

Then there was Amy, sweet adorable little Amy. He'd feed her to the seagulls. Maybe that would shut them up, and it would definitely shut the little gullible chatterbox up. Couldn't follow her sisters around if she was in pieces being flown around the coast. Imagine the quiet of shutting the kids up, *and* sending the seagulls away. Maybe then Joe could enjoy his holiday. Not that this was his holiday, it was his daughter's and *her* family's holiday. He was just a fucking babysitter who was coerced into coming; bitch may as well have held him at gunpoint. All he wanted to do was sit in peace at home remembering the life he had, and should still be having if the cruel ruthless world hadn't snatched it from him.

The voice inside Joe reminded him of that over and over. A broken record, but stuck on the part it needed him to hear.

*"This world has taken everything from you, and now look how they're treating you."*

He'd lost the person who mattered most to him, and for no reason. Just out of the blue. One minute it's holiday websites with warm hugs and beautiful smiles while they considered the next stage of their life together, the next moment it's hospital corridors. Cold sterile rooms with the joy sucked out of them. Machines that angrily rumbled as they tried to rescue what couldn't be saved. Voices constantly saying how sorry they were, but there was nothing more they could do. How was that fair? How did they spend all that time together to have it extinguished so suddenly? Wasn't cancer care meant to be advanced now? How could she die within two months? What the fuck.

And now he was left with these mini-reminders of a life he no longer wanted. A bunch of ungrateful kids who wanted nothing more than to mock him or chat to their friends when they're meant to be on holiday with their family. They even took their fucking tablets to the restaurant last night! What the hell is that all about? Again, his daughter ensured him it was fine as Kate watched some stupid fucking talking doll bullshit on the tablet while rolling her eyes at him. Amy was glued to her dumb fucking pig. Hayley took multiple pictures of her food; when did that become a thing? Meanwhile he'd worked hard his entirely life and had nothing left, couldn't even spend one measly year retired with his wife.

These ungrateful little fucks didn't deserve to live. They had no clue what life was, how hard it could be, and how unfair it turned out. The game of life was rigged; he'd be doing them a favour putting them out of their misery early. Well, except Kate; that wouldn't be a favour. He'd make her suffer; no way was she getting off lightly. The darkness inside him nodded in agreement as an evil smile graced Joe's lips and he wiped away the tears that had been freely flowing from his disturbed eyes. Then he remembered he should be counting.

"Forty-two... Forty-three... Forty-four..."

"You count so slowly Grandpa," Kate whinged like the little cunt she was. Couldn't even let him count in his own time, what a bitch. He was going to enjoying destroying, brutalising, and humiliating her. His mind started thinking what else he could do; she needed to suffer. The other two he'd kill relatively quickly after a little fun, but he'd draw Kate out. A quick death was too good for that one. He'd teach her some fucking manners, some respect for her elders. He'd make her cry, beg, plead, and promise to be the good little girl she once was, and then he'd roll his eyes at her. He laughed out loud at the thought.

"Grandpa are you finding us or not?" Kate asked. Well, demanded really.

*For fucksakes, he thought.* Such a rush to die.

"Forty-eight... Forty-nine... Fifty... Ready or not here I come."

As Grandpa Joe struggled to his feet with half his face rotting under his mammoth beard, the door to the caravan swung open. Mike's annoying voice broke Joe's stride as he was setting off to hunt down and annihilate the grandkids. Without thinking, he made a beeline for his daughter's prick of a husband instead. Joe slammed the caravan door in Mike's face as he greeted him. That wiped the stupid fucking grin from his mouth, which was no doubt stuck up his daughter's cunt minutes earlier. *How dare he.*

Mike stumbled back down the small set of steps leading to the caravan door with his nose bent out of shape and leaking blood on the worn grass beneath. The seagulls were already eyeing up the crimson snack. Sarah was further back, unloading something from the car, completely unaware of the attack. When she made her way to the caravan, she saw Joe on top of Mike. At first she thought Mike must have slipped on the steps, and her dad was helping him up. She'd warned the kids countless times not to run up them as they were slippery with all the rain which plagued their getaway, but then she saw what was really going on.

Joe had bit into Mike's neck and was ripping his throat out. As impossible as the view was, that's exactly what was happening. She saw thick veins pulsating from the side of her dad's neck under his skin, but saw them in full view from her husband. Veins, tendons, bone, the whole lot were on display as Joe bit and clawed through her husband's neck like an animal that hadn't eaten for a week now successfully digging for food. Mike didn't put up much of a fight as Joe somehow easily overpowered him. Mike wasn't a big guy, but he was bigger and younger than Joe, yet at no point could he tip the frail old man off him.

His cries were short lived as Joe stopped any sounds reaching his mouth. He may not have had the opportunity to cut the windpipe from any of the kids, but had bitten through Mike's. Sarah screamed, before charging forward and barging her savage father from her dying husband. It was too late. Blood continued to flow from the countless open wounds around Mike's throat and face as Sarah tried in vain to stop the leaks with her hands. There were simply to many to plug.

Joe looked confused as he watched Sarah sitting beside him in tears. As she stared back at him, he looked like her dad again, rather than whatever had torn into her husband. She didn't have time to work out what the fuck had happened. Sarah rushed inside the caravan screaming for her kids, and locked the door. Joe laid in the blood-soaked grass wondering what he'd done as the realisation of his action hit, while the seagulls squawked around him, already picking at Mike's remains.

*

Joe tried explaining the brief madness to the officers when they arrived and roughly cuffed him after witnessing the appalling sight of Mike's corpse on the ground. Joe couldn't comprehend his own words but told them about the twisted demonic voice inside him that somehow made him kill Mike, and almost butcher his beautiful granddaughters. He thought they'd think he was a fucking lunatic and lock him away for life, but they shared a curious glace like they somehow believed him.

It didn't matter to Joe whether they believed him or not; the damage was already done. He'd killed his daughter's husband, taking away her partner like life had cruelly done to him. He understood a lot of her pain, but he'd lost his beloved to an unrelenting disease, not his own fucking father's bloodthirsty hands while still being so young. He was ashamed.

He'd never be able to forgive himself, and Sarah certainly would never be able to forgive him, demonic presence or not. His three innocent grandkids would grow up without a father, the fourth would never even see their father's face in person. Hayley already knew what he'd done; she'd seen the end of it through the caravan window when she heard her mum's screams. There'd be no more dancing in her future, and he was the cause of that.

Joe wanted to die. He wanted to be with April again, but knew his kind-hearted wife would be up in the clouds where she belonged, and when his time came, he'd be even further away from her, in the fiery pits of hell reunited with that demonic voice.

# Heather Trent MP

Heather dreamt of the day she'd have the stage, like the Secretary of State for Transportation currently had. While she found most of what he was saying utterly boring, and it had nothing to do with her so she didn't give a shit, she did want the time and position he had to talk. She aspired for a higher role than just an elected local MP. She needed to be part of the cabinet one day; fuck, she needed to be Prime Minister one day. It wasn't so far-fetched either, but it also wasn't easy. She had to play the game and side with the right people. *Even politics has its politics*, she smirked to herself.

She sat in the House of Commons listening to him rabbit on about taxes, the state of the roads, and all the other monotonous bullshit that came with the role, while wondering what route she'd take. Heather saw herself initially maybe being the Secretary of State for Education, that would be fun. Or maybe the Health Minister. Both roles required a shit ton of hard work and public relations, but they were good stepping stones to the number one position. Maybe she could be Mayor somewhere important? But Mayor roles always required staying for a length of time. She preferred the idea of the revolving carousel that was the Secretary of whatever-the-fuck.

Heather had won her elected position by a landslide, but that was partly down to the lack of opposition, and being on the right side in her area. They always voted Conservative, it was a given. If she won with anything less than a landslide it would have been a failure, so the achievement meant very little, but that didn't mean it couldn't be spun. Everything had an angle. Everything was about how you presented it. Statistics could say whatever you wanted them to say if you approached it from the right point of view. Yes, she should have won by a big margin, and did, but she was the youngest winner of that seat to date.

The first female elected in that area. Had a bigger margin than the previous representative. There was always an angle to play with, and Heather was becoming a student of the game.

For the moment, she had to sit several rows back from the top government officials and roles, and slightly further back still from the PM and cabinet, but she was making her way forward. Two years ago she was in the bleachers, so far back into the backbenches that you couldn't even see her on the tele. Now her face would randomly appear over the shoulders of more important people, but you could see her. *Baby steps*, although Heather didn't think of it in such childish terms. She was on the advance. This was war, and she was gaining territory, and support. The amount of fuck-ups and drop outs in the party meant a new position was never too far away; she just had to keep her nose clean and be ready.

She was definitely ready, but as far as keeping her nose clean, there were one or two indiscretions that needed forgetting. Like practically every other politician in the country, she hadn't covered herself in glory during the expense scandal, but she was young, dumb, and practically unknown when it happened. Enough time had passed that the British public didn't bring it up as often anymore. Time heals all wounds, *even political scandal*. She hadn't learnt to cover her tracks as well back then, and that new kitchen wasn't going to build itself. Plus, others in higher positions and under more scrutiny had done worse.

Then there was the whole fucking a married man thing. That sort of shit was still looked down upon in the eyes of the British public despite divorce rates being sky high and celebrity scandal being a past-time. She was happily married now with a little baby at home, so figured that would hopefully help clean up her public image. Her husband was almost as boring as the Secretary of Transport, but he was a good looking guy with money and connections, so aided her public persona.

The public didn't need to know about the other affairs and kinky shit she was into; that could all be kept under wraps. She was older and wiser now, with a better team around her. Damage control was big business in politics, and there were plenty of experts in the field. She felt covered and protected in that department, so Heather just needed to continue doing her job well. She needed to make the right impression, dazzle the right people, and maybe make the odd big statement here and there to raise her profile and public awareness. Most importantly in the modern climate, Heather just needed to keep the fuck out of trouble.

*"This is so fucking boring,"* a voice reaffirmed inside her head as she continued to listen to the 'right honourable this and that.' But, oddly, the voice wasn't Heather's. She wasn't quite sure what it was. It didn't feel like an inner-monologue, but it was expressing her own feelings. She instantly recognised it as something corrupt and morally bankrupt, but also couldn't help but admire its power. Colour her intrigued.

*"It should be you up there."* Darkness dripped from its words, every one of them laced with poison and malicious intent. There was also wisdom in the words, and knowing, but its evil could already be felt in Heather's stomach. Whatever this voice was, it wasn't here to truly help her.

"I will be one day," Heather replied steadfast to the voice inside. She didn't say it aloud but anyone watching her on TV would have seen the movement on her lips, and the uncomfortable expression on her face. They may have also spotted the beginnings of the rot spreading from the bottom of her neck. It looked like popping veins at first, like those transformation scenes in movies when someone is getting powers for the first time, or running out of air. Heather felt like she was on the receiving end of both as she felt slight movement and a weird burning sensation on her neck. To the touch, it wasn't burning, however; if anything, it felt mushy.

"What are you doing to me?" she asked, using her inside voice, rather than freaking out and saying it loudly for all around her to hear. She was freaking out, big time, but couldn't lose her shit in the middle of Parliament. Fuck, she'd never live that down. Never get primed for a big role or elected as Prime Minister. She'd be a sideshow oddball at best. Tabloid cannon fodder. They'd probably start using her as an example for some mental health campaign, which, while raising her public awareness, would all but end her career. No, she couldn't act fucking crazy and start shouting at the voice inside her gut, whether it was there or not.

*"I'm helping you,"* the voice offered. *"Giving you power,"* it suggested, but couldn't hide its utter disdain of her.

"You don't want to help me, you want to use me."

*"Can't the two be the mutually beneficial?"* it smugly hissed.

Fuck, that voice was pure evil, Heather thought. She'd heard rumblings from various higher ups about something happening in the country. That there'd been some odd reports of late about an evil presence, something about dark voices and rotting faces. It all sounded like mumbo-jumbo when Heather first heard it, but already she knew it had to be real. It was happening to her right now, and in the middle of Parliament of all places.

"Please," she begged of the darkness at the realisation of what it was, or at least what it was capable of. "I don't want to hurt anyone." That wasn't exactly true; Heather had a nasty streak to her, and there were plenty she would harm given the discreet chance, but if what she heard about the demonic voice was indeed true, then this was a whole other level of wickedness. The things she'd heard were beyond evil; they were ungodly, and cruel to the very core. She'd snuff out a reporter or two given the opportunity, maybe an ex here or there, but she didn't want to fucking demolish and eat people.

The voice mocked her with its putrid laugh, something Heather was not accustomed to. She wanted to scold the evil presence, but instead was looking for the exits while a new speaker addressed the House. She couldn't even focus on who it was, just that there was movement in front of her. She ducked her head, looking half asleep as she spotted a nearby camera angling in her direction. That wouldn't look great on the television, but it was better than everyone seeing the rot spread across her face. She considered asking those around her for help, but while they were colleagues, they were also in competition with one another. Politics was *Battle Royale*, and if she asked for help she'd be eliminated for good. No, she needed to deal with this herself, and the best way was to get the hell out of there.

But Heather couldn't move, or open her mouth; the Rot had somehow sewn it shut. It no longer felt like anyone else was in the large chamber. As the decay took to her eyes, it was just her and the voice privately conversing.

*"I think it's time to announce my presence,"* the Rot confided in Heather.

"Please…" was all she could think in return, but the Rot wasn't interested in her pathetic pleas. It didn't give the slightest fuck about her career, her family, her little baby at home waiting for its mummy. Heather barely gave a fuck about the rugrat, so why should the Rot? It told her as much, and while she vehemently denied it, it wasn't wrong.

*"This will advance your career,"* the voice told her. Although its persuasive tone was drenched in sin, the voice was getting through to Heather. She wanted to fight it, knew what it would ask of her was wrong on every possible level, but yet… that initial intrigue she had was starting to blossom, even if it was against her will.

*"There will be several new openings,"* the voice sneered as it

allowed Heather to look through her eyes once more.

She took in the sights of the rich and powerful in front of her. All held positions she wanted because all were sitting closer to the Prime Minster than her. She'd take any single one of their jobs in an instant, given the chance.

*"I'm offering you that chance."*

She didn't have to know or care what the job entailed. Health, Education, Treasury, all meant a bigger title, more power. One step closer to the ultimate role of leading the country. But while their titles held more perceived power than hers, she was the one with the actual power. She could feel the monstrous strength flowing through her tainted veins.

"What is this?" she asked, this time aloud, but no one paid her any attention. *They soon would be.* The Rot didn't need to answer, as Heather already knew what it was: it was undiluted strength. A dark, unrelenting force that could destroy anything in its path. True power. An ancient evil the likes of which the world wasn't ready for, but it was ready for the world. It needed to be unleashed, to continue its reclaim. The Rot was a million miles away from the end game, but it was ready to step up and make itself known, and Heather was the vehicle chosen for the grand gesture.

*"Take what's yours,"* the voice commanded. *"They're all beneath you. The front row has your name etched into it. Claim it!"* The voice shouted the last part and lit something dark and primal inside Heather as the Rot seized full control of her face. Whatever little subtlety it had used in the past, there was no need for now. Giant scabs and scars spread across her raw cheeks and nose. Her eyes fell back into her head. making her look blind despite seeing clearer than ever. Big slices of skin began to peel from her degraded face, hanging loosely like a decomposing corpse. A dry itchiness took over, but when Heather held her hands to her face, it felt wet and soggy like her

face was crumbling. The sight was amplified and horrific, but she couldn't see it, nor had any inclination to look. It served a purpose, and that purpose was to spread fear throughout the room.

It was an odd sight for the handful of viewers watching at home, and an almost comical sight for the members of Parliament in attendance. Which, once again, was far less than there should have been - although for once that would be a good thing. Heather oddly rose from her seated position and stood with her now untied hair draped across her face like fucking Sadako. When she brushed her hair back, the stifled laughter rippling through the few observing her became an audible gasp. The thoughts of 'what's she doing?' changed to 'what the fuck!'

A couple of them, like Heather, had heard the ridiculous noise through the grapevine and their minds instantly wondered whether this was what people were talking about, because the rot on Heather's face looked absolutely fucking foul. Most of them in attendance had seen and greeted her earlier in the day, and she didn't look like this before the session began. Heather was a beautiful looking woman for a politician and a rising star within the party, so she wasn't someone they ignored, even if her position still didn't merit much fanfare. But now... now she had their undivided attention for all the wrong reasons.

Heather let out an animalistic ear-piecing shriek before she dove onto the MP in front of her and sank her teeth deep into the woman's stern face, biting her long nose clean off. The woman barely had time to cry out before flopping off her seat to the bloody chamber floor as Heather tore into more of her face. A senior MP tried to fight Heather off as she came for him next, but she overpowered him with ease and snapped his neck before the live feed could be cut. It left the viewers at home wondering whether some fucking bizarre eighteen certificated found footage horror was playing during the day time. Ofcom was going to get some complaints.

Pandemonium swept the prestigious room as security left its position on the various exits. Some headed towards the Prime Minister and focused on his protection while the rest made their way towards Heather. Too many MPs were scrambling for the exits for security to be able to take her down, or even reach her. No one had a clear sight as Heather's rampage continued.

Heather snapped arms and legs from those trying to flee. Bit into faces and chewed eyeballs and noses. She grabbed the Secretary of State for Transport as he tried to hide behind a young backbencher and punched her fist into his mouth. Heather forced her hand deeper and deeper into the Minister's throat as he gagged for air. If she could have ripped out his fucking insides, or pulled his heart back out through his mouth, she would have. Unfortunately, that wasn't how the human body worked, so she settled for ripping his tonsils and tongue out and shoving them up his fucking nose. Not that that was remotely normal either; the force running through her truly was remarkable.

*"The new Secretary of State for Transport, Mrs Heather Trent,"* the voice inside gleefully announced as she ripped up part of the bench and bashed the ever-loving fuck out of her next victim. Heather left the ex-Minster crumpled on the floor with half his face splattered across the famous green furnishing. Security escorted the PM out of the room and closed the heavy doors behind them, much to the dismay of several more members of Parliament narrowing in on the same door. They'd have to find another exit. Their screams intensified as they watched their deranged colleague, who some previously considered a friend, rip apart half the fucking party and opposition.

As a bunch of self serving assholes, they'd all struggled to get the fuck out of there and had trampled over one another and pushed each other into Heather's path to create more distance.

Now they had to witness their own cowardice and see the results of throwing their fellow party members under the bus. It really had turned into the survival of the fittest Heather had predicted, and the exact reason she hadn't asked for help.

A bullet exploded into Heather's shoulder as a member of security finally got a clean shot. He didn't want to shoot with the amount of innocent people around, but Heather was still clearly going fucking berserk and needed to be stopped. She'd killed or injured far too many already and no-one seemed to be able to get close to her. It was like one of those movie scenes where fate conspired to stop the hero reaching the victim in time. The officer who fired his gun wondered if that was exactly what was happening as the brief sight of Heather closed in again and she vanished back into the crowd of desperate escapees.

The bullet didn't stop Heather in the slightest. All it managed to do was spin her around and direct her attention towards another MP. *They all looked the same to her at this point.* All just meat ready to be expired. The voice inside her head was in a full blown frenzy. It cheered her on with all its evil might. It could feel the hate, the power, the fear running through the prominent room. It saw and smelt the lives being brutally taken all for its own pleasure and need. Its vehicle was unstoppable, and starting to enjoy herself, whether though her own will or not. Carnage and chaos reigned supreme within the darkness that had taken control of the famous building. Fuck, the Rot needed this.

"*More,*" it demanded of its meat mech. The Rot wasn't in complete control but had all the influence. It switched off any ideas of pain Heather might have and directed her to the next victim. Another bite of the throat. Another neck snapped. More fingers through the eyes and hair scalped from the latest victim as two more shots ploughed through her. A fourth bullet blew a hole in one of her own eyes, rendering it completely fucking useless as it dripped from the blood-soaked socket upon her decaying face. The bullet had come from above her near the backbenches as security climbed higher for a better opportunity. It meant they had that better shot, but also meant the trajectory of the bullet missed Heather's brain as she stumbled forward to cause more death and depravity.

Almost everyone left alive had escaped the room as Heather dropped her final victim to the floor, having torn his cock off through his expensive trousers and started eating it while his piss still leaked from the mutilated appendage. She hadn't had much time for that sort of barbarism in her rage, but, sensing he was probably her last victim, she made the most of it. The security team surrounded Heather with their guns raised. They were shouting some instructions at her but Heather's hearing was gone. She could only see through one eye and her body was absolutely spent. She could barely stand, let alone pay attention to their demands.

With her final breath, Heather lunged forward and received twenty-six bullets in her head and body; they weren't taking prisoners. The Rot laughed harder and harsher than ever before as the decay dissolved from Heather's decimated face and its voice faded from within her. That was an all you could eat buffet and it could already feel the results. It would let the aftermath settle for a bit, but fuck, the Rot felt more powerful than ever now. It felt like it was evolving.

*

Fourteen MPs died that day with another forty suffering some sort of injuries either at Heather's hands, or their fellow party and opposition members as everyone tried to get out of there. The public feed hadn't lasted long enough for the country to witness the devastation in full, but they'd seen enough and heard the impossible reports.

It was said that Heather went mad, but others stepped forward telling how they'd seen and heard of similar things in recent weeks. This wasn't madness, this was something all together more frightening. This was hatred and darkness beyond all comprehension, evil in its purest form. The Devil's work. This was a crisis. The country may have grown tired of the word pandemic, but this wickedness was spreading and it could affect anyone without warning. What other cases were there that no one knew about? How long had this been happening? Who would it happen to next?

The whole country was on edge, and so it fucking should be...

The End

# BOOKS BY STEPHEN COOPER

Abby Vs The Splatploitation Brothers
Hillbilly Farm

Near Death

Blood-Soaked Wrestling

The Rot

Check out all my work at
www.Splatploitation.com
And find me on YouTube

Splatploitation
Press

Printed in Great Britain
by Amazon